"Listen, you want to talk about that kiss? We kissed. It was nothing we hadn't done before."

Of course this kiss was so, so much more than she was letting on. *Damn it.*

"But I'm not the same girl you used to know," she continued, propping her hand on her hip. "I'm not looking for a relationship. I'm not looking for love. I'm not even interested in you anymore, Will."

Cat nearly choked on that lie, but mentally applauded herself for the firmness in her delivery and for stating all she needed to. She wasn't about to start playing whatever game Will had in mind because she knew one thing for certain...she'd lose.

Will stepped closer, took hold of her wrist and pulled her arm gently behind her back. Her body arched into his as she gripped her feather duster and tried to concentrate on the bite of the handle into her palm and not the way those mesmerizing eyes were full of passion and want.

"Not interested?" he asked with a smirk. "You may be able to lie to yourself, Cat, but you can never lie to me. I know you too well."

* * *

Maid for a Magnate is part of the series
Dynasties: The Montoros—One royal family
must choose between love and destiny!

Dear Reader,

You've made it to book five of the Montoro family saga! At least, I hope you've read the first four, because the plot thickens! Royalty, betrayal, secret affairs...what more could you want in a Harlequin Desire story? Oh, right, a hunky hero with redeeming qualities and a heroine who makes him work for love.

Are you ready for Will and Catalina's second-chance story? These two have quite a bit to overcome, other than just the fact she's the maid for his father. Maybe a little time stranded on a secluded beach will help them face their past and force true feelings to the surface. I love the way Will is persistent, yet still vulnerable where Cat is concerned. He's ready to fight for what he wants, and he wants this woman.

I truly hope you're enjoying the Montoro family's story, and I cannot wait for you to meet Will and Catalina. This dynamic couple deserves their happily-ever-after!

Happy reading,

Jules

MAID FOR
A MAGNATE

———

JULES BENNETT

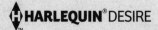

Special thanks and acknowledgment are given to Jules Bennett
for her contribution to the Dynasties: The Montoros miniseries.

ISBN-13: 978-0-373-73410-8

Maid for a Magnate

Recycling programs
for this product may
not exist in your area.

Printed in U.S.A.

Award-winning author **Jules Bennett** is no stranger to romance—she met her husband when she was only fourteen. After dating through high school, the two married. He encouraged her to chase her dream of becoming an author. Jules has now published nearly thirty novels. She and her husband are living their own happily-ever-after while raising two girls. Jules loves to hear from readers through her website, julesbennett.com, her Facebook fan page or on Twitter.

Books by Jules Bennett

Harlequin Desire

What the Prince Wants
A Royal Amnesia Scandal
Maid for a Magnate

The Barrington Trilogy

When Opposites Attract...
Single Man Meets Single Mom
Carrying the Lost Heir's Child

Harlequin Special Edition

The St. Johns of Stonerock

Dr. Daddy's Perfect Christmas
The Fireman's Ready-Made Family
From Best Friend to Bride

Visit the Author Profile page at Harlequin.com or julesbennett.com for more titles.

A huge thanks to the Harlequin Desire team
for including me in this amazing continuity.
And a special thanks to Janice, Kat,
Katherine, Andrea and Charlene.
I loved working with you all on this project.

One

JUAN CARLOS SALAZAR II TRUE HEIR
TO THRONE

Will Rowling stared at the blaring headline as he sipped his coffee and thanked every star in the sky that he'd dodged marrying into the royal family of Alma. Between the Montoro siblings and their cousin Juan Carlos, that was one seriously messed up group.

Of course his brother, James, had wedded the beautiful Bella Montoro. Will's father may have had hopes of Will and Bella joining forces, but those devious plans obviously had fallen through when James fell in love with Bella instead.

Love. Such a fickle thing that botched up nearly every best laid plan. Not that Will had ever been on board with the idea of marrying Bella. He'd rather remain single than marry just to advance his family's business interests.

The Montoros were a force to be reckoned with in Alma, now that the powerful royal family was being restored to the throne after more than seventy years in exile. And Patrick Rowling was all too eager to have his son marry into such prestige, but thankfully that son was not to be Will.

Bella's brother had been heading toward the throne, until shocking letters were discovered in an abandoned family farmhouse, calling into question the lineage of the Montoros and diverting the crown into the hands of their cousin.

Secrets, scandal, lies… Will was more than happy to turn the reins over to his twin.

And since Will was officially single, he could carry out his own devious plan in great detail—his plot didn't involve love but a whole lot of seduction.

First, though, he had to get through this meeting with his father. Fortunately, Will's main goal of taking back control of his life involved one very intriguing employee of his father's household so having this little meeting at the Rowling home in Playa del Onda instead of the Rowling Energy offices was perfectly fine with him. Now that James had married and moved out and Patrick was backing away from working as much, Patrick used his weekend home more often.

"Rather shocking news, isn't it?"

Still clutching the paper in one hand and the coffee mug in the other, Will turned to see his father breeze into the den. While Patrick leaned more toward the heavier side, Will prided himself on keeping fit. It was just another way he and his father were different though some around them felt Will was a chip off the old block.

At one time Will would've agreed with those people, but he was more than ready to show everyone, including his father, he was his own man and he was taking charge.

"This bombshell will certainly shake things up for Alma." Will tossed the newspaper onto the glossy mahogany desktop. "Think parliament will ratify his coronation?"

Patrick grunted as he sank into his leather desk chair. "It's just a different branch of the Montoro family that will be taking the throne, so it really doesn't matter."

Will clutched his coffee cup and shook his head. Anything to do with the Montoros was not his problem. He had his own battles to face, starting with his father right now.

"What did you need to see me so early about?" his father asked, leaning back so far in the chair it squeaked.

Will remained standing; he needed to keep the upper hand here, needed to stay in control. Even though he was going up against his father's wishes, Will had to take back control of his own life. Enough with worrying about what his father would say or do if Will made the wrong move.

James had never bowed to their father's wishes and Will always wondered why his twin was so against the grain. It may have taken a few years to come around, but Will was more than ready to prove himself as a formidable businessman.

Will was a master at multitasking and getting what he wanted. And since he'd kissed Cat a few weeks ago, he'd thought of little else. He wanted her…and he would have her. Their intense encounter would allow for nothing less.

But for right this moment, Will was focusing on his

new role with Rowling Energy and this meeting with his father. Conquering one milestone at a time.

"Up till now, you've had me dealing with the company's oil interests," Will stated. "I'm ready to take total control of the real estate division, too."

His father's chest puffed out as he took in a deep breath. "I've been waiting for you to come to me with this," Patrick said with a smile. "You're the obvious choice to take over. You've done a remarkable job increasing the oil profits. They're up twelve percent since you put your mark on the company."

Will intended to produce financial gains for all of the company's divisions. For years, he'd wanted to get out from under his father's thumb and take control, and now was his chance. And that was just the beginning of his plans where Rowling Energy was concerned.

Finally, now that Will was seeing clearly and standing on his own two feet, nothing would stand in his way. His father's semiretirement would just help ease the path to a beautiful life full of power and wealth... and a certain maid he'd set in his sights.

"I've already taken the liberty of contacting our main real estate clients in London," Will went on, sliding his hands into his pockets and shifting his weight. "I informed them they would be dealing with me."

Will held his father's gaze. He'd taken a risk contacting the other players, but Will figured his father would be proud and not question the move. Patrick had wanted Will to slide into the lead role of the family business for years. Slowly Will had taken over. Now he was ready to seal every deal and hold all the reins.

"Another man would think you're trying to sneak behind his back." Patrick leaned forward and laced his fingers together on the desktop. "I know better. You're taking charge and that's what I want. I'll make sure my assistant knows you will be handling the accounts from here on out. But I'm here anytime, Will. You've been focused on this for so long, your work has paid off."

Will nodded. Part one of his plan was done and had gone just as smoothly as he'd envisioned. Now he needed to start working on the second part of his plan. And both aspects involved the same tactic…trust. He needed to gain and keep the trust of both his father and Cat or everything would blow up in his face.

Will refused to tolerate failure on any level.

Especially where Cat was concerned. That kiss had spawned an onslaught of emotions he couldn't, wouldn't, ignore. Cat with her petite, curvy body that fit perfectly against his. She'd leaned into that kiss like a woman starved and he'd been all too happy to give her what she wanted.

Unfortunately, she'd dodged him ever since. He didn't take that as a sign of disinterest. Quite the opposite. If she wasn't interested, she'd act as if nothing had happened. But the way she kept avoiding him when he came to visit his father at the Playa del Onda estate only proved to Will that she was just as shaken as he was. There was no way she didn't feel something.

Just one kiss and he had her trembling. He'd use that to his advantage.

Seeing Cat was another reason he opted to come to his father's second home this morning. She couldn't avoid him if he cornered her at her workplace. She'd been the maid for his twin brother, James, but James had often been away playing football—or as the Yanks called it, soccer—so Cat hadn't been a temptation thrust right in Will's face. But now she worked directly under Patrick. Her parents had also worked for Patrick, so

Cat had grown up around Will and James. It wasn't that long ago that Will had set his sights on Cat. Just a few years ago, in fact, he'd made his move, and they'd even dated surreptitiously for a while. That had ended tragically when he'd backed down from a fight in a moment of weakness. Since their recent kiss had brought back their scorching chemistry, Will knew it was time for some action.

Will may have walked out on her four years ago, but she was about to meet the new Will…the one who fought for what he wanted. And he wanted Cat in his bed and this time he wouldn't walk away.

Will focused back on his father. "I'll let myself out," he stated, more than ready to be finished with this part of his day. "I'll be in touch once I hear back from the investors and companies I contacted."

Heading for the open double doors, Will stopped when his father called his name.

"You know, I really wanted the thing with you and Bella to work," Patrick stated, as he stared at the blaring, boldface headline.

"She found love with my brother. She and I never had any type of connection. You'd best get used to them together."

Patrick focused his attention back on Will. "Just keep your head on your shoulders and don't follow the path your brother has. Getting sidetracked isn't the way to make Rowling Energy grow and prosper. Just do what you've been doing."

Oh, he intended to do just that.

Will gave his father a brief nod before heading out into the hallway. Little did his father know, Will was fully capable of going after more than one goal at a time. He had no intention of letting the oil or real estate businesses slide. If anything, Will fully intended to expand both aspects of the business into new territory within the next year.

Will also intended to seduce Cat even sooner. Much sooner. And he would stop at nothing to see all of his desires fulfilled.

That familiar woodsy scent assaulted her...much like the man himself had when he'd kissed her a few weeks ago.

Could such a full-on assault of the senses be called something so simple as a kiss? He'd consumed her from the inside out. He'd had her body responding within seconds and left her aching and wanting more than she should.

Catalina kept her back turned, knowing full well who stood behind her. She'd managed to avoid running into him, though he visited his father more and more lately. At this point, a run-in was inevitable.

She much preferred working for James instead of Patrick, but now that James was married, he didn't stay here anymore and Patrick did. Catalina had zero tolerance for Patrick and the fact that she worked directly for him now only motivated her more to finish saving up to get out of Alma once and for all. And the only reason she was working for Patrick was because she needed the money. She knew she was well on her way to leaving, so going to work for another family for only a few months didn't seem fair.

Years ago her mother had moved on and still worked for a prestigious family in Alma. Cat prayed her time here with Patrick was coming to an end, too.

But for now, she was stuck here and she hadn't been able to stop thinking about that kiss. Will had silently taken control of her body and mind in the span of just a few heated moments, and he'd managed to thrust her directly into their past to the time when they'd dated.

Unfortunately, when he'd broken things off with her, he'd hurt her more than she cared to admit. Beyond leaving her when she hadn't even seen it coming, he'd gone so far as to say it had all been a mistake. His exact words, which had shocked her and left her wondering how she'd been so clueless. Catalina wouldn't be played for a fool and she would never be his "mistake" again. She had more pride than that…even if her heart was still bruised from the harsh rejection.

Even if her lips still tingled at the memory of their recent kiss.

Catalina continued to pick up random antique trin-kets on the built-in bookshelves as she dusted. She couldn't face Will, not just yet. This was the first en-counter since that night three weeks ago. She'd seen him, he'd purposely caught her eye a few times since then, but he'd not approached her until now. It was as if the man enjoyed the torture he inflicted upon her senses.

"You work too hard."

That voice. Will's low, sultry tone dripped with sex appeal. She didn't turn around. No doubt the sight of him would still give her that swift punch of lust to the gut, but she was stronger now than she used to be…or she'd been stronger before he'd weakened her defenses with one simple yet toe-curling kiss.

"Would that make you the pot or the kettle?" she asked, giving extra attention to one specific shelf be-cause focusing on anything other than this man was all that was holding her sanity together.

His rich laughter washed over her, penetrating any

defense she'd surrounded herself with. Why did her body have to betray her? Why did she find herself drawn to the one man she shouldn't want? Because she hadn't forgotten that he'd recently been the chosen one to wed Bella Montoro. Bella's father had put out a false press release announcing their engagement, but of course Bella fell for James instead and Will ended up single. James had informed Cat that Bella and Will were never actually engaged, but still. With Will single now, and after that toe-curling kiss, Cat had to be on her guard. She had too much pride in herself to be anybody's Plan B.

"That spot is clean." His warm, solid hand slid easily onto her shoulder. "Turn around."

Pulling in a deep breath, Catalina turned, keeping her shoulders back and her chin high. She would not be intimidated by sexy good looks, flawless charm and that knowing twinkle in Will's eye. Chemistry wouldn't get her what she wanted out of life…all she'd end up with was another broken heart.

"I have a lot on my list today." She stared at his ear, trying to avoid those piercing aqua eyes. "Your dad should be in his den if you're looking for him."

"Our business is already taken care of." Will's hand dropped, but he didn't step back; if anything, he shifted closer. "Now you and I are going to talk."

"Which is just another area where we differ," she retorted, skirting around him to cross in front of the mantel and head to the other wall of built-in bookcases. "We have nothing to discuss."

Of course he was right behind her. The man had dropped her so easily four years ago yet in the past few weeks, he'd been relentless. Perhaps she just needed to be more firm, to let him know exactly where she stood.

"Listen." She spun back around, brandishing her feather duster at him. Maybe he'd start sneezing and she could make a run for it. "I've no doubt you want to talk about that kiss. We kissed. Nothing we hadn't done before."

Of course this kiss was so, so much more; it had penetrated to her very soul. Dammit.

"But I'm not the same girl you used to know," she continued, propping her hand on her hip. "I'm not looking for a relationship, I'm not looking for love. I'm not even interested in you anymore, Will."

Catalina nearly choked on that lie, but she mentally applauded herself for the firmness in her delivery and for stating all she needed to. She wasn't about to start playing whatever game Will had in mind because she knew one thing for certain…she'd lose.

Will stepped closer, took hold of her wrist and pulled her arm gently behind her back. Her body arched into his as she gripped her feather duster and tried to concentrate on the bite of the handle into her palm and not the way those mesmerizing eyes were full of passion and want.

"Not interested?" he asked with a smirk. "You may be able to lie to yourself, Cat, but you can never lie to me. I know you too well."

She swallowed. "You don't know me at all if you think I still like to be called Cat."

Will leaned in until his lips caressed the side of her ear. "I want to stand out in your mind," he whispered. "I won't call you what everyone else does because our relationship is different."

"We have nothing but a past that was a mistake." She purposely threw his words back in his face and she didn't care if that was childish or not.

Struggling against his hold only caused her body to respond even more as she rubbed against that hard, powerful build.

"You can fight this all you want," he said as he eased back just enough to look into her eyes. "You can deny you want me and you can even try to tell yourself you hate me. But know this. I'm also not the same man I used to be. I'm not going to let you get away this time."

Catalina narrowed her gaze. "I have goals, Will, and you're not on my list."

A sultry grin spread across his face an instant before he captured her lips. His body shifted so that she could feel just how much he wanted her. Catalina couldn't stop herself from opening her mouth for him and if her hands had been free, she probably would've fully embarrassed herself by gripping his hair and holding him even tighter.

Damn this man she wanted to hate, but couldn't.

He demanded her affection, demanded desire from her and she gave it. Mercy, she had no choice.

He nipped at her, their tongues tangling, before he finally, finally lifted his head and ran a thumb across her moist bottom lip.

"I have goals, too, Cat," he murmured against her mouth. "And you're on the top of *my* list."

The second he released her, she had to hurry to steady herself. By the time she'd processed that full-on arousing attack, Will was gone.

Typical of the man to get her ready for more and leave her hanging. She just wished she still wasn't tingling and aching all over for more of his touch.

Two

Will sat on his patio, staring down at his boat and contemplating another plan of action. Unfortunately his cell phone rang before he could fully appreciate the brilliant idea he'd just had.

His father's name popped up on the screen and Will knew without answering what this would be about. It looked as if Patrick Rowling had just got wind of Will's latest business actions.

"Afternoon," he greeted, purposely being more cheerful than he assumed his father was.

"What the hell are you doing with the Cortes Real Estate company?"

Will stared out onto the sparkling water and crossed his ankles as he leaned back in his cushioned patio chair. "I dropped them."

"I'm well aware of that seeing as how Dominic called me to raise hell. What were you thinking?" his father demanded. "When you steamrolled into the head position, I thought you'd make wise moves to further the family business and make it even more profitable into the next generation. I never expected you to sever ties with companies we've dealt with for decades."

"I'm not hanging on to business relationships based on tradition or some sense of loyalty," Will stated, refusing to back down. "We've not gained a thing in the past five years from the Corteses and it was time to cut our losses. If you and Dom want to be friends, then go play golf or something, but his family will no longer do business with mine. The bottom line here is money, not hurt feelings."

"You should've run this by me, Will. I won't tolerate you going behind my back."

Will came to his feet, pulled in a deep breath of ocean air and smiled because he was in charge now and his father was going to start seeing that the "good" twin wasn't always going to bend and bow to Patrick's wishes. Will was still doing the "right thing," it just so happened the decisions made were Will's version of right and not his father's.

"I'm not sneaking at all," Will replied, leaning against the scrolling wrought iron rail surrounding his deck. "I'll tell you anything you want to know, but since I'm in charge now, I'm not asking for permission, either."

"How many more phone calls can I expect like the one I got from Cortes?"

His father's sarcasm wasn't lost on Will.

"None for the time being. I only let one go, but that doesn't mean I won't cut more ties in the future if I see we aren't pulling any revenue in after a period of time."

"You run your decisions by me first."

Giving a shrug even though his father couldn't see him, Will replied, "You wanted the golden son to take over. That's exactly what I'm doing. Don't second-guess me and my decisions. I stand to gain or lose like you do and I don't intend to see our name tarnished. We'll come out on top if you stop questioning me and let me do this job the way it's meant to be done."

Patrick sighed. "I never thought you'd argue with me."

"I'm not arguing. I'm telling you how it is."

Will disconnected the call. He wasn't going to get into a verbal sparring match with his father. He didn't have time for such things and nothing would change Will's mind. He'd gone over the numbers and cross-referenced them for the past years. Though that was a job his assistant could easily do, Will wanted his eyes on every report since he was taking over. He needed to know exactly what he was dealing with and how to plan accordingly.

His gaze traveled back to his yacht nestled against his private dock. Speaking of planning accordingly, he had more personal issues to deal with right now. Issues that involved one very sexy maid.

It had taken a lifeless, arranged relationship with Bella to really wake Will up to the fact his father had his clutches so tight, Will had basically been a marionette his entire life. Now Will was severing those strings, starting with the ridiculous notion of his marrying Bella.

Will was more than ready to move forward and take all the things he'd been craving: money and Cat. A beautiful combo to start this second stage of his life.

And it would be soon, he vowed to himself as he stalked around his outdoor seating area and headed inside. Very soon he would add to his millions, secure his place as head of the family business by cementing its leading position in the oil and real estate industries and have Cat right where he wanted her…begging.

Catalina couldn't wait to finish this day. So many things had come up that hadn't been on her regular schedule…just another perk of working for the Rowling patriarch. She had her sights set on getting home, taking off her ugly, sensible work shoes and digging into another sewing project that would give her hope, get her one step closer to her ultimate goal.

This next piece she'd designed late last night would be a brilliant, classy, yet fun outfit to add to her private collection. A collection she fully intended to take with her when she left Alma very soon.

Her own secret goal of becoming a fashion designer had her smiling. Maybe one day she could wear her own stylish clothes to work instead of boring black cotton pants and button-down shirt with hideous shoes. Other than her mother, nobody knew of Catalina's real dream, and she had every intention of keeping things that way. The last thing she needed was anyone trying to dissuade her from pursuing her ambitions or telling her that the odds were against her. She was fully aware of the odds and she intended to leap over them and claim her dream no matter how long it took. Determination was a hell of a motivator.

She came to work for the Rowlings and did her job— and that was about all the human contact she had lately. She'd been too wrapped up in materials, designs and fantasies of runway shows with her clothing draped on models who could fully do her stylish fashions justice.

Not that Catalina hated how she looked, but she

wasn't blind. She knew her curvy yet petite frame wasn't going to get her clothing noticed. She merely wanted to be behind the scenes. She didn't need all the limelight on her because she just wanted to design, no more.

As opposed to the Rowling men who seemed to crave the attention and thrive on the publicity and hoopla.

Adjusting the fresh arrangement of lilacs and white calla lilies in the tall, slender crystal vase, Catalina placed the beautiful display on the foyer table in the center of the open entryway. There were certain areas where Patrick didn't mind her doing her own thing, such as choosing the flowers for all the arrangements. She tended to lean toward the classy and elegant…which was the total opposite of the man she worked for.

James on the other hand had more fun with her working here and he actually acknowledged her presence. Patrick only summoned her when he wanted to demand something. She hated thinking how much Will was turning into his father, how business was ruling him and consuming his entire life.

Will wasn't in her personal life anymore, no matter how much she still daydreamed about their kisses. And Patrick would only be her employer for a short time longer. She was hoping to be able to leave Alma soon, leave behind this life of being a maid for a man she didn't care for. At least James was pleasant and a joy to work for. Granted, James hadn't betrayed Cat's mother the way Patrick had. And that was just another reason she wanted out of here, away from Patrick and the secret Cat knew about him.

Catalina shoved those thoughts aside. Thinking of all the sins from Patrick's past wouldn't help her mood.

Patrick had been deceitful many years ago and Catalina couldn't ignore her mother's warning about the Rowling men. Even if Will had no clue how his father had behaved, it was something Catalina would never forget. She was only glad she'd found out before she did something foolish like fall completely in love with Will.

Apparently the womanizing started with Patrick and trickled down to his sons. James had been a notorious player before Bella entered his life. After all, there was nothing like stealing your twin brother's girl, which is what James had done to Will. But all had worked out in the end because Bella and James truly did love each other even if the way they got there was hardly normal. Leave it to the Rowlings and the Montoros to keep life in Alma interesting.

Catalina just wished those recent kisses from Will weren't overriding her mother's sound advice and obvious common sense.

Once the arrangement was to her liking—because perfection was everything whether you were a maid or a CEO—Catalina made her way up the wide, curved staircase to the second floor. The arrangements upstairs most likely needed to be changed out. At the very least, she'd freshen them up with water and remove the wilting stems.

As she neared the closed door of the library, she heard the distinct sound of a woman sobbing. Catalina had no clue who was visiting. No women lived here, and she'd been in the back of the house most of the morning and hadn't seen anyone come in.

The nosy side of her wanted to know what was going on, but the employee side of her said she needed to mind her own business. She'd been around the Rowling family enough to know to keep her head down, do her job and remember she was only the help.

Inwardly she groaned. She hated that term. Yes, she was a maid, but she was damn good at her job. She took pride in what she did. No, cleaning toilets and washing sheets wasn't the most glam of jobs, but she knew what she did was important. Besides, the structure and discipline of her work was only training her for the dream job she hoped to have someday.

The rumble of male voices blended in with the female's weeping. Whatever was going on, it was something major. Catalina approached the circular table in the middle of the wide hall. As she plucked out wilted buds here and there, the door to the library creaked open. Catalina focused on the task at hand, though she was dying to turn to see who came from the room.

"Cat."

She cringed at the familiar voice. Well, part of her curiosity was answered, but suddenly she didn't care what was going on in that room. She didn't care who Will had in there, though Catalina already felt sorry for the poor woman. She herself had shed many tears over Will when he'd played her for a fool, getting her to think they could ignore their class differences and have a relationship. "I need to see you for a minute."

Of course he hadn't asked. Will Rowling didn't ask... he demanded.

Stiffening her back, she expected to see him standing close, but when she turned to face him, she noted he was holding onto the library door, with only the top half of his body peeking out of the room.

"I'm working," she informed him, making no move to go see whatever lover's spat he was having with the unknown woman.

"You need to talk to Bella."

Bella? Suddenly Catalina found herself moving down

the hall, but Will stepped out, blocking her entry into the library. Catalina glanced down to his hand gripping her bicep.

"Her aunt Isabella passed away in the middle of the night," he whispered.

Isabella Montoro was the grand matriarch of the entire Montoro clan. The woman had been around forever. Between Juan Carlos being named the true heir to the throne and now Isabella's death, the poor family was being dealt one blow after another.

Will rubbed his thumb back and forth over Catalina's arm. "You know Bella enough through James and I figured she'd want another woman to talk to. Plus, I thought she could relate to you because…"

Swallowing, she nodded. When she and Will had dated briefly, Catalina had just lost her grandmother, a woman who had been like a second mother to her. Will had seen her struggle with the loss…maybe the timing of the loss explained why she'd been so naïve to think she and Will could have a future together. For that moment in time, Catalina had clung to any hope of happiness and Will had shown her so much…but it had all been built on lies.

Catalina started to move by him, but his grip tightened. "I don't want to bring up bad memories for you." Those aqua eyes held her in place. "As much as Bella is hurting, I won't sacrifice you, so tell me if you can't go in there."

Catalina swallowed as she looked back into those eyes that held something other than lust. For once he wasn't staring at her as if he wanted to rip her clothes off. He genuinely cared or at least he was playing the part rather well. Then again, he'd played a rather impressive role four years ago pretending to be the doting boyfriend.

Catalina couldn't afford to let her guard down. Not again with this man who still had the power to cripple her. That kiss weeks ago only proved the control he still had and she'd never, ever let him in on that fact. She could never allow Will to know just how much she still ached for his touch.

"I'll be fine," she replied, pulling her arm back. "I'd like to be alone with her, though."

Will opened his mouth as if to argue, but finally closed it and nodded.

As soon as Catalina stepped inside, her heart broke. Bella sat in a wingback chair. James rested his hip on the arm and Bella was curled into his side sobbing.

"James." Will motioned for his twin to follow him out.

Leaning down, James muttered something to Bella. Dabbing her eyes with a tissue, Bella looked up and saw she had company.

Catalina crossed to the beautiful woman who had always been known for her wild side. Right now she was hurting over losing a woman who was as close as a mother to her.

The fact that Will thought Catalina could offer comfort, the fact that he cared enough to seek her out, shouldn't warm her heart. She couldn't let his moment of sweetness hinder her judgment of the man. Bella was the woman he'd been in a relationship with only a month ago. How could Catalina forget that? No matter the reasons behind the relationship, Catalina couldn't let go of the fact that Will would've said *I do* to Bella had James not come along.

Will had an agenda, he always did. Catalina had no

clue what he was up to now, but she had a feeling his newfound plans included her. After all this time, was he seriously going to pursue her? Did he honestly think they'd start over or pick up where they'd left off?

Catalina knew deep down he was only after one thing…and she truly feared if she wasn't careful, she'd end up giving in.

Three

Will lifted the bottle of scotch from the bar in the living room, waving it back and forth slightly in a silent invitation to his brother.

James blew out a breath. "Yeah. I could use a drink."

Neither mentioned the early time. Sometimes life's crises called for an emergency drink to take the edge off. And since they'd recently started building their relationship back up, Will wanted to be here for his brother because even though Bella was the one who'd suffered the loss, James was no doubt feeling helpless.

"Smart thinking asking Catalina to help." James took the tumbler with the amber liquid and eased back on the leather sofa. "Something going on there you want to talk about?"

Will remained standing, leaning an elbow back against the bar. "Nothing going on at all."

Not to say there wouldn't be something going on very

soon if he had his way about it. Those heated kisses only motivated him even more…not to mention the fact that his father would hate knowing "the good twin" had gone after what he wanted, which was the total opposite of Patrick's wishes.

James swirled the drink as he stared down into the glass. "I know Isabella has been sick for a while, but still, her death came as a shock. Knowing how strong-willed she was, I'd say she hung on until Juan Carlos was announced the rightful heir to the throne."

Will nodded, thankful they were off the topic of Cat. She was his and he wasn't willing to share her with anyone right now. Only a month ago, Bella had caught Will and Cat kissing, but at the time she'd thought it was James locking lips with the maid. The slight misunderstanding had nearly cost James the love of his life. "How is Bella dealing with the fact her brother was knocked off the throne before he could fully take control?"

The Montoro family was being restored to the Alma monarchy after decades of harsh dictatorship. First Rafael Montoro IV and then, when he abdicated, his brother Gabriel were thought to be the rightful heirs. However, their sister, Bella, had then uncovered damning letters in an old family farmhouse, indicating that because of a paternity secret going back to before World War II, Juan Carlos's line of the family were the only legitimate heirs.

"I don't think that title ever appealed to Gabriel or Bella, to be honest." James crossed his ankle over his knee and held onto his glass as he rested it on the arm of the sofa. "Personally, I'm glad the focus is on Juan Carlos right now. Bella and I have enough media attention as it is."

In addition to the fact that James had married a member of Alma's royal family, he was also a star football player who drew a lot of scrutiny from the tabloids. The newlyweds no doubt wanted some privacy to start building their life together, especially since James had also recently taken custody of his infant baby, Maisey—a child from a previous relationship.

"Isabella's passing will have the media all over the Montoros and Juan Carlos. I'm probably going to take Bella and Maisey back to the farmhouse to avoid the spotlight. The renovations aren't done yet, but we need the break."

"What can I do to help?" Will asked.

James tipped back the last of the scotch, and then leaned forward and set the empty tumbler on the coffee table. "Give me back that watch," he said with a half smile and a nod toward Will's wrist.

"Nah, I won this fair and square," Will joked. "I told you that you wouldn't be able to resist putting a ring on Bella's finger."

James had inherited the coveted watch from their English grandfather and wore it all the time. It was the way people told the twins apart. But Will had wanted the piece and had finally won it in a bet that James would fall for Bella and propose. Ironically, it had almost ended James and Bella's relationship because Will had been wearing the watch that night he'd kissed Cat in the gazebo. Bella had mistaken him for James and jumped to conclusions.

"Besides the watch, what else can I do?" Will asked.

"I have no idea." James shook his head and blew out a sigh. "Right now keeping Dad out of my business would be great."

Will laughed. "I don't think that will be a problem.

He's up in arms about some business decisions I've made, so the heat is off you for now."

"Are you saying the good twin is taking charge?"

"I'm saying I'm controlling my own life and this is only the first step in my plan."

Leaning forward, James placed his elbows on his knees. "Sounds like you may need my help. I am the black sheep, after all. Let me fill you in on all the ways to defy our father."

"I'm pretty sure I'm defying him all on my own." Will pushed off the bar and shoved his hands in his pockets. "I'll let you know if I need any tips."

James leveled his gaze at Will. "Why do I have a feeling this new plan of yours has something to do with the beautiful maid?"

Will shrugged, refusing to rise to the bait.

"You were kissing her a few weeks ago," James reminded him. "That little escapade nearly cost me Bella."

The entire night had been a mess, but thankfully things ultimately worked out the way they should have.

"So Catalina..."

Will sighed. "You won't drop it, will you?"

"We practically grew up together with her, you dated before, you were kissing a few weeks ago. I'm sure dear old Dad is about to explode if you are making business decisions that he isn't on board with and if you're seducing his maid."

"I'm not seducing anyone." Yet. "And what I do with my personal life is none of his concern."

"He'll say different once he knows you're after the maid. He'll not see her as an appropriate match for you," James countered, coming to his feet and glancing toward the ceiling as if he could figure out what was going on upstairs between the women. "What's taking them so long? Think it's safe to go back?"

Will nodded. "Let's go see. Hopefully Cat was able to calm Bella down."

"Cat, huh?" James smiled as he headed toward the foyer and the staircase. "You called her that years ago and she hated it. You still going with that?"

Will patted his brother on the shoulder. "I am going for whatever the hell I want lately."

And he was. From this point on, if he wanted it, he was taking it…that went for his business and his bedroom.

The fact that the maid was consoling a member of the royal family probably looked strange from the outside, and honestly it felt a bit weird. But Catalina had been around Bella enough to know how down-to-earth James's wife was. Bella never treated Catalina like a member of the staff. Not that they were friends by any means, but Catalina was comfortable with Bella and part of her was glad Will had asked her to come console Bella over the loss of her aunt.

"You're so sweet to come in here," Bella said with a sniff.

Catalina fought to keep her own emotions inside as she hugged Bella. Even though years had passed, Catalina still missed her grandmother every single day. Some days were just more of a struggle than others.

"I'm here anytime." Catalina squeezed the petite woman, knowing what just a simple touch could do to help ease a bit of the pain, to know you weren't alone in your grief. "There will be times memories sneak up on you and crush you all over again and there will be days you are just fine. Don't try to hide your emotions.

Everyone grieves differently so whatever your outlet is, it's normal."

Bella shifted back and patted her damp cheeks. "Thank you. I didn't mean to cry all over you and bring up a bad time in your life."

Pushing her own memories aside, Catalina offered a smile. "You didn't do anything but need a shoulder to cry on. I just hope I helped in some small way to ease the hurt and I'm glad I was here."

"Bella."

The sound of James's voice had Catalina stepping back as he came in to stand beside his wife. Tucking her short hair behind her ears, Catalina offered the couple a brief smile. James hugged Bella to his side and glanced at Catalina.

"I didn't want to interrupt, but I know you need to work, too," James said. "We really appreciate you."

Those striking Rowling eyes held hers. This man was a star athlete, wanted by women all over the world. Yet Catalina felt nothing. He looked exactly like Will, but in Catalina's heart…

No. Her heart wasn't involved. Her hormones were a jumbled mess, but her heart was sealed off and impenetrable…at least where Will was concerned. Maybe when she left Alma she'd settle somewhere new and find the man she was meant to be with, the man who wouldn't consider her a mistake.

Those damning words always seemed to be in the forefront of her mind.

"I'm here all day through the week," Catalina told Bella. "You can always call me, too. I'm happy to help any way I can."

"Thank you." Bella sniffed. She dabbed her eyes again and turned into James's embrace.

Catalina left the couple alone and pulled the door shut behind her. She leaned against the panel, closed her eyes and tipped her head back. Even though Catalina still had her mother, she missed her grandmother. There was just something special about a woman who enters your life in such a bold way that leaves a lasting impression.

Catalina knew Bella was hurting over the loss of her aunt, there was no way to avoid the pain. But Bella had a great support team and James would stay by her side.

A stab of remorse hit her. Bella's and Catalina's situations were so similar, yet so different. Will had comforted her over her loss when they'd first started dating and Catalina had taken his concern as a sign of pure interest. Unfortunately, her moments of weakness had led her to her first broken heart.

The only good thing to come out of it was that she hadn't given him her innocence. But she'd certainly been tempted on more than one occasion. The man still tempted her, but she was smarter now, less naïve, and she had her eyes wide open.

Pushing off the door, she shoved aside the thoughts of Will and their past relationship. She'd jumped from one mistake to another after he broke things off with her. Two unfortunate relationships were more than enough for her. Focusing on turning her hobby and passion for making clothes into a possible career had kept her head on straight and her life pointed in the right direction. She didn't have time for obstacles…no matter how sexy.

She made her way down the hall toward the main bathroom on the second floor. This bathroom was nearly the size of her little flat across town. She could afford something bigger, but she'd opted to keep her place small because she lived alone and she'd rather save her money for fabrics, new sewing machines, investing in her future and ultimately her move. One day that nest egg she'd set aside would come in handy and she couldn't wait to leave Alma and see how far her dreams could take her. Another couple months and she truly believed she would be ready. She still couldn't pinpoint her exact destination, though. Milan was by far the hot spot for fashion and she could head there and aim straight for the top. New York was also an option, or Paris.

Catalina smiled at the possibilities as she reached beneath the sink and pulled out fresh white hand towels. Just as she turned, she collided with a very hard, very familiar chest.

Will gripped her arms to steady her, but she wasn't going anywhere, not when she was wedged between his solid frame and the vanity biting into her back.

"Excuse me," she said, gripping the terrycloth next to her chest and tipping her chin up. "I'm running behind."

"Then a few more minutes won't matter." He didn't let up on his hold, but instead leaned back and kicked the door shut with his foot. "You're avoiding me."

Hadn't she thought this bathroom was spacious just moments ago? Because now it seemed even smaller than the closet in her bedroom.

"Your ego is getting in the way of common sense," she countered. "I'm working. Why are you always here lately anyway? Don't you have an office to run on the other side of town?"

The edge of his mouth kicked up in a cocky half smile. "You've noticed. I was beginning to think you were immune."

"I've been vaccinated."

Will's rich laugh washed over her and she cursed the goose bumps that covered her skin. Between his touch, his masculine scent and feeling his warm breath on her, her defenses were slipping. She couldn't get sucked back into his spell, not when she was so close to breaking free once and for all.

"Come to dinner with me," he told her, smile still in place as if he truly thought she'd jump at the chance. "Your choice of places."

Now Catalina laughed. "You're delusional. I'm not going anywhere with you."

His eyes darkened as they slid to her lips. "You will."

Catalina pushed against him, surprised when he released her and stepped back. She busied herself with changing out the hand towels on the heated rack. Why wouldn't he leave? Did he not take a hint? Why suddenly was he so interested in her when a few years ago she'd been "a mistake"? Plus, a month ago he'd almost been engaged to another woman.

Being a backup plan for anybody was never an option. She'd rather be alone.

Taking more care than normal, Catalina focused on making sure the edges of the towels were perfectly lined up. She needed to keep her shaking hands busy.

"You can't avoid this forever." Will's bold words sliced through the tension. "I want you, Cat. I think you know me well enough to realize I get what I want."

Anger rolled through her as she spun around to face him. "For once in your life, you're not going to be able to have something just because you say so. I'm not just a possession, Will. You can't buy me or even work your charm on me. I've told you I'm not the same naïve girl I used to be."

In two swift steps, he'd closed the gap between them

and had her backed against the wall. His hands settled on her hips, gripping them and pulling them flush with his. This time she didn't have the towels to form a barrier and his chest molded with hers. Catalina forced herself to look up into his eyes, gritted her teeth and prayed for strength.

Leaning in close, Will whispered, "I'm not the man I used to be, either."

A shiver rippled through her. No, no he wasn't. Now he was all take-charge and demanding. He hadn't been like this before. He also hadn't been as broad, as hard. He'd definitely bulked up in all the right ways…not that she cared.

"What would your father say if he knew you were hiding in the bathroom with the maid?" she asked, hoping the words would penetrate through his hormones. He'd always been yanked around by Daddy's wishes… hence their breakup, she had no doubt.

Will shifted his face so his lips were a breath away from hers as his hands slid up to her waist, his thumbs barely brushing the underside of her breasts. "My father is smart enough to know what I'd be doing behind a closed door with a sexy woman."

Oh, man. Why did she have to find his arrogance so appealing? Hadn't she learned her lesson the first time? Wanting Will was a mistake, one she may never recover from if she jumped in again.

"Are you saying you're not bowing down to your father's commands anymore? How very grown up of you."

Why was she goading him? She needed to get out of here because the more he leaned against her, the longer he spoke with that kissable mouth so close to hers, the harder he was making her life. Taunting her, making her ache for things she could never have.

"I told you, I'm a different man." His lips grazed hers as he murmured, "But I still want you and nobody is going to stand in my way."

Why did her hormones and need for his touch override common sense? Letting Will kiss her again was a bad, bad idea. But she couldn't stop herself and she'd nearly arched her body into his just as he stepped back. The heat in his eyes did nothing to suppress the tremors racing through her, but he was easing backward toward the closed door.

"You're leaving?" she asked. "What is this, Will? A game? Corner the staff and see how far she'll let me take things?"

He froze. "This isn't a game, Cat. I'm aching for you, to strip you down and show you exactly what I want. But I need you to literally hurt for wanting me and I want you to be ready. Because the second I think we're on the same level, you're mine."

And with that, he turned and walked out, leaving the door open.

Catalina released a breath she hadn't realized she'd been holding. How dare he disrupt her work and get her all hot and bothered? Did he truly think she'd run to him begging to whisk her off to bed?

As much as her body craved his touch, she wouldn't fall into his bed simply because he turned on the sex appeal. If he wanted her, then that was his problem.

Unfortunately, he'd just made his wants her problem as well because now she couldn't think of anything else but how amazing he felt pressed against her.

Catalina cursed herself as she gathered the dirty towels. If he was set on playing games, he'd chosen the wrong opponent.

Four

Catalina lived for her weekends. Two full days for her to devote to her true love of designing and sewing. There was nothing like creating your own masterpieces from scratch. Her thick portfolio binder overflowed with ideas from the past four years. She'd sketched designs for every season, some sexy, some conservative, but everything was timeless and classy in her opinion.

She supposed something more than just heartache and angst had come from Will's exiting her life so harshly. She'd woken up, finally figured out what she truly wanted and opted to put herself, her dreams as top priority. And once she started achieving her career goals, she'd work on her personal dreams of a family. All of those were things she couldn't find in Alma. This place had nothing for her anymore other than her mother, who worked for another family. But her mother had already said she'd follow Catalina wherever she decided to go.

Glancing around, Catalina couldn't remember where she put that lacy fabric she'd picked up in town a few weeks ago. She'd seen it on the clearance table and had nothing in mind for it at the time, but she couldn't pass up the bargain.

Now she knew exactly what she'd use the material for. She had the perfect wrap-style dress in mind. Something light and comfortable, yet sexy and alluring with a lace overlay. The time would come when Catalina would be able to wear things like that every single day. She could ditch her drab black button-down shirt and plain black pants. When she dressed for work every morning, she always felt she was preparing for a funeral.

And those shoes? She couldn't wait to burn those hideous things.

Catalina moved around the edge of the small sofa and thumbed through the stack of folded materials on the makeshift shelving against the wall. She'd transformed this spare room into her sewing room just last year and since then she'd spent nearly all of her spare time in the cramped space. One day, though... One day she'd have a glorious sewing room with all the top-notch equipment and she would bask in the happiness of her creations.

As she scanned the colorful materials folded neatly on the shelves, her cell rang. Catalina glanced at the arm of the sofa where her phone lay. Her mother's name lit up the screen.

Lunging across the mess of fabrics on the cushions, Catalina grabbed her phone and came back to her feet as she answered.

"Hey, Mum."

"Sweetheart. I'm sorry I didn't call earlier. I went out to breakfast with a friend."

Catalina stepped from her bedroom and into the cozy

living area. "No problem. I've been sewing all morning and lost track of time."

"New designs?" her mother asked.

"Of course." Catalina sank down onto her cushy sofa and curled her feet beneath her. "I actually have a new summery beach theme I'm working on. Trying to stay tropical and classy at the same time has proven to be more challenging than I thought."

"Well, I know you can do it," her mother said. "I wore that navy-and-gray-print skirt you made for me to breakfast this morning and my friend absolutely loved it. I was so proud to be wearing your design, darling."

Catalina sat up straighter. "You didn't tell her—"

"I did not," her mother confirmed. "But I may have said it was from a new up-and-coming designer. I couldn't help it, honey. I'm just so proud of you and I know you'll take the fashion world by storm once you leave Alma."

Just the thought of venturing out on her own, taking her secret designs and her life dream and putting herself out there had a smile spreading across her face as nerves danced in her belly. The thought of someone looking over her designs with a critical eye nearly crippled her, but she wouldn't be wielding toilet wands for the rest of her life.

"I really think I'll be ready in a couple of months," Catalina stated, crossing back to survey her inventory on the shelves. "Saying a timeframe out loud makes this seem so real."

Her mother laughed. "This is your dream, baby girl. You go after it and I'll support you all the way. You know I want you out from under the Rowlings' thumb."

Catalina swallowed as she zeroed in on the lace and

pulled it from the pile. "I know. Don't dwell on that, though. I'm closer to leaving every day."

"Not soon enough for me," her mother muttered.

Catalina knew her mother hated Patrick Rowling. Their affair years ago was still a secret and the only reason Catalina knew was because when she'd been dumped by Will and was sobbing like an adolescent schoolgirl, her mother had confessed. Maria Iberra was a proud woman and Catalina knew it had taken courage to disclose the affair, but Maria was dead set on her daughter truly understanding that the Rowling men were only after one thing and they were ruthless heartbreakers. Feelings didn't exist for those men, save for James, who seemed to be truly in love and determined to make Bella happy.

But Patrick was ruthless in everything and Will had followed suit. So why was he still pursuing her? She just wanted a straight answer. If he just wanted sex, she'd almost wish he'd just come out and say it. She'd take honesty over adult games any day.

Before she could respond to her mother, Catalina's doorbell rang. "Mum, I'll call you back. Someone is at my door."

She disconnected the call and pocketed her cell in her smock pocket. She'd taken to wearing a smock around her waist to keep pins, thread, tiny scissors and random sewing items easily accessible. Peeking through the peephole, Catalina only saw a vibrant display of flowers.

Flicking the deadbolt, she eased the door open slightly. "Yes?"

"Catalina Iberra?"

"That's me."

The young boy held onto the crystal vase with two hands and extended it toward her. "Delivery for you."

Opening the door fully, she took the bouquet and soon realized why this boy had two hands on it. This thing was massive and heavy.

"Hold on," she called around the obscene arrangement. "Let me give you a tip."

"Thank you, ma'am, but that was already taken care of. You have a nice day."

Catalina stepped back into her apartment, kicked the door shut with her foot and crossed the space to put the vase on her coffee table. She stood back and checked out various shades and types of flowers. Every color seemed to be represented in the beautiful arrangement. Catalina couldn't even imagine what this cost. The vase alone, made of thick, etched glass, appeared to be rather precious.

A white envelope hung from a perfectly tied ribbon around the top of the vase. She tugged on the ribbon until it fell free and then slid the small envelope off. Pulling the card out and reading it, her heart literally leapt up into her throat. *Think of me. W.*

Catalina stared at the card, and then back at the flowers. Suddenly they weren't as pretty as they'd been two minutes ago. Did he seriously think she'd fall for something as cliché as flowers? Please. And that arrogant message on the card was utterly ridiculous.

Think of him? Lately she'd done little else, but she'd certainly never tell him that. What an ego he'd grown since they were last together. And she thought it had been inflated then.

But because no one was around to see her, she bent down and buried her face in the fresh lilacs. They smelled so wonderful and in two days they would still look amazing.

A smile spread across her face as her plan took shape. Will had no idea who he was up against if he thought an expensive floral arrangement was going to get her to drop her panties or common sense.

As much as she was confused and a bit hurt by his newfound interest in her now that he wasn't involved with Bella, she had to admit, toying with him was going to be fun. Only one person could win this battle…she just prayed her strength held out and she didn't go down in the first round.

Will slid his cell back into his pocket and leaned against the window seat in his father's office at his Playa del Onda home. "We've got them."

Patrick blinked once, twice, and then a wide smile spread across his face. "I didn't think you could do it."

Will shrugged. "I didn't have a doubt."

"I've been trying to sign with the Cherringtons for over a year." Patrick shook his head and pushed off the top of his desk to come to his feet. "You're really making a mark here, Will. I wondered how things would fair after Bella, but business is definitely your area of expertise."

Will didn't tell his father that Mrs. Cherrington had tried to make a pass at Will at a charity event a few months back. Blackmail in business was sometimes not a bad thing. It seemed that Mrs. Cherrington would do anything to keep her husband from learning she'd had too much to drink and gotten a little frisky. She apparently went so far as to talk him into doing business with the Rowlings, but considering both families would prosper, Will would keep her little secret.

In Will's defense, he didn't let her advances go far. Even if she weren't old enough to be his mother and if she hadn't smelled as if she bathed in a distillery, she was married. He may not want any part of marriage for himself, but that didn't mean he was going to home in on anybody else's, either.

Before he could say anything further, Cat appeared in the doorway with an enormous bouquet. The arrangement reminded him of the gift he'd sent her. He'd wondered all weekend what she'd thought of the arrangement. Had she smiled? Had she thought about calling him?

He'd end this meeting with his father and make sure to track her down before he headed back to the Rowling Energy offices for an afternoon meeting. He had an ache that wasn't going away anytime soon and he was starting to schedule his work around opportunities to see Cat. His control and priorities were becoming skewed.

"I'm sorry to interrupt," she stated, not glancing Will's way even for a second. "I thought I'd freshen up your office."

Patrick glanced down at some papers on his desk and motioned her in without a word. Will kept his eyes on Cat, on her petite, curvy frame tucked so neatly into her black button-down shirt and hip-hugging dress pants. His hands ached to run over her, *sans* clothing.

She was sporting quite a smirk, though. She was up to something, which only put him on full alert.

"I don't always keep flowers in here, but I thought this bouquet was lovely." She set it on the accent table nestled between two leather wingback chairs against the far wall. "I received these the other day and they just did a number on my allergies. I thought about trashing them, but then realized that you may want something fresh for your office, Mr. Rowling."

Will stood straight up. She'd received those the other day? She'd brought his bouquet into his father's office and was giving it away?

Apparently his little Cat had gotten feisty.

"I didn't realize you had allergies," Will stated, drawing her attention to him.

She tucked her short black hair behind her ears and smiled. "And why should you?" she countered with a bit more sass than he was used to from her. "I'll leave you two to talk."

As she breezed out just as quickly as she'd come, Will looked at his father, who was staring right back at him with a narrowed gaze. Why did Will feel as if he'd been caught doing something wrong?

"Keep your hands off my staff," his father warned. "You already tried that once. I hesitated keeping her on, but James swore she was the best worker he'd ever had. Her mother had been a hard worker, too, so don't make me regret that decision."

No way in hell was he letting his father, or anybody else for that matter, dictate what he could and couldn't do with Cat. Listening to his father's instructions about his personal life was what got Will into this mess in the first place.

"Once we've officially signed with the Cherringtons, I'll be sure to send them a nice vintage wine with a personalized note."

Patrick came to his feet, rested his hands on his desk and leaned forward. "You're changing the subject."

"The subject of your staff or my personal life has no relevance in this meeting," Will countered. "I'll be sure to keep you updated if anything changes, but my assistant should have all the proper paperwork emailed by the end of the day."

Will started to head out the door, but turned to glance over his shoulder. "Oh, and the next time Cat talks to you, I suggest you are polite in return and at least look her in the eye."

Leaving his father with his mouth wide open, Will turned and left the office. Perhaps he shouldn't have added that last bit, but Will wasn't going to stand by and watch his father dismiss Cat like that. She was a person, too—just because she cleaned for Patrick and he signed her checks didn't mean he was more important than she. Will had no doubt that when Cat worked for James, he at least treated her with respect.

Dammit. Why was he getting so defensive? He should be pissed she'd dumped his flowers onto his father. There was a twisted irony in there somewhere, but Will was too keyed up to figure it out. What was it about her blatantly throwing his gift back in his face that had him so turned on?

Will searched the entire first and second floors, but Cat was nowhere to be found. Granted, the house was twelve thousand square feet, but there weren't that many people on staff. How could one petite woman go missing?

Will went back to the first floor and into the back of the house where the utility room was. The door was closed and when he tried to turn the knob, he found it locked. That was odd. Why lock a door to the laundry? He heard movement, so someone was in there.

He tapped his knuckles on the thick wood door and waited. Finally the click of a lock sounded and the door eased open. Cat's dark eyes met his.

"What do you want?" she asked.

"Can I come in?"

"This isn't a good time."

He didn't care if this was good or bad. He was here and she was going to talk to him. He had to get to another meeting and wasn't wasting time playing games.

Will pushed the door, causing her to step back. Squeezing in, he shut the door behind him and flicked the lock into place.

Cat had her back to him, her shoulders hunched. "What do you want, Will?"

"You didn't like the flowers?" he asked, crossing his arms over his chest and leaning against the door.

"I love flowers. I don't like your clichéd way of getting my attention or trying to buy me."

He reached out, grabbed her shoulder and spun her around. "Look at me, dammit."

In an instant he realized why she'd been turned away. She was clutching her shirt together, but the swell of her breasts and the hint of a red lacy bra had him stunned speechless.

"I was trying to carry a small shelf into the storage area and it got caught on my shirt," she explained, looking anywhere but at his face as she continued to hold her shirt. "I ran in here because I knew there was a sewing kit or maybe even another shirt."

Everything he'd wanted to say to her vanished from his mind. He couldn't form a coherent thought at this point, not when she was failing at keeping her creamy skin covered.

"I'd appreciate it if you'd stop staring," she told him, her eyes narrowing. "I don't have time for games or a pep talk or whatever else you came to confront me about. I have work to do and boobs to cover."

Her snarky joke was most likely meant to lighten the mood, but he'd wanted her for too long to let anything deter him. He took a step forward, then another, until he'd backed her up against the opposite wall. With her hands holding tight onto her shirt, her eyes wide and her cheeks flushed, there was something so wanton yet innocent about her.

"What do you like?" he asked.

Cat licked her lips. "What?" she whispered.

Will placed a hand on the wall, just beside her head, and leaned in slightly. "You don't like flowers. What do you like?"

"Actually, I love flowers. I just took you for someone who didn't fall into clichés." She offered a slight smile, overriding the fear he'd seen flash through her eyes moments ago. "But you're trying to seduce the maid, so maybe a cliché is all we are."

Will slid his other hand across her cheek and into her hair as he brought his mouth closer. "I don't care if you're the queen or the maid or the homeless person on the corner. I know what I want and I want you, Cat."

She turned her palms to his chest, pushing slightly, but not enough for him to think she really meant for him to step back…not when she was breathless and her eyes were on his mouth.

"I'm not for sale," she argued with little heat behind her words.

He rubbed his lips across hers in a featherlight touch that instantly caused her to tremble. That had to be her body, no way would he admit those tremors were from him.

"Maybe I'll just sample, then."

Fully covering her mouth, Will kept his hand fisted in her hair as he angled her head just where he wanted it. If she didn't want him at all, why did she instantly open for him?

The sweetest taste he'd ever had was Cat. No woman compared to this one. As much as he wanted to strip her naked right here, he wanted to savor this moment and simply savor her. He wanted that familiar taste only Cat could provide, he wanted to reacquaint himself with every minute sexy detail.

Delicate hands slid up his chest and gripped his shoulders, which meant she had to have released her hold on her shirt. Will removed his hand from the wall and gripped her waist as he slid his hand beneath the hem of her shirt and encountered smooth, warm skin. His thumb caressed back and forth beneath the lacy bra.

Cat arched into him with a slight moan. Her words may have told him she wasn't interested, but her body had something else in mind...something much more in tune with what he wanted.

Will shifted his body back just enough to finish un-buttoning her shirt. He parted the material with both hands and took hold of her breasts. The lace slid beneath his palm and set something off in him. His Cat may be sweet, somewhat innocent, but she loved the sexy lingerie. Good to know.

Reluctantly breaking the kiss, Will ached to explore other areas. He moved down the column of her throat and continued to the swell of her breasts. Her hands slid into his hair as if she were holding him in place. He sure as hell wasn't going anywhere.

Will had wanted this, wanted her, four years ago. He'd wanted her with a need that had only grown over the years. She'd been a virgin then; he'd known it and respected her for her decisions. He would've waited for her because she'd been so special to him.

Then his father had issued an ultimatum and Will had made the wrong choice. He didn't fight for what he wanted and he'd damn well never make that mistake again.

Now Cat was in his arms again and he'd let absolutely nothing stand in the way of his claiming her.

"Tell me you want this," he muttered against her heated skin. "Tell me."

His hands encircled her waist as he tugged her harder against his body. Will lifted his head long enough to catch the heat in her eyes, the passion.

A jiggling of the door handle broke the spell. Will stepped back as Cat blinked, glanced down and yanked her shirt together.

"Is someone in there?" a male voice called.

Cat cleared her throat. "I got something on my shirt," she called back. "Just changing. I'll be out shortly, Raul."

Will stared down at her. "Raul?" he whispered.

Cat jerked her shirt off and stalked across the room. Yanking open a floor-to-ceiling cabinet, she snagged another black shirt and slid into it. As she secured the buttons, she spun back around.

"He's a new employee, not that it's any of your business." When she was done with the last button, she crossed her arms over her chest. "What just happened here, as well as in the bathroom the other day, will not happen again. You can't come in to where I work and manhandle me. I don't care if I work for your family. That just makes this even more wrong."

Will couldn't suppress the grin. "From the moaning, I'd say you liked being manhandled."

He started to take a step forward but she held up her hand. "Don't come closer. You can't just toy with me, Will. I am not interested in a replay of four years ago. I have no idea what your agenda is, but I won't be part of it."

"Who says I have an agenda?"

Her eyes narrowed. "You're a Rowling. You all have agendas."

So she was a bit feistier than before. He always loved a challenge—it was impossible to resist.

"Are you still a virgin?"

Cat gasped, her face flushed. "How dare you. You have no right to ask."

"Considering I'm going to take you to bed, I have every right."

Cat moved around him, flicked the lock and jerked the door open. "Get the hell out. I don't care if this is your father's house. I'm working and we are finished. For good."

Will glanced out the door at a wide-eyed Raul. Before he passed, he stopped directly in front of Cat. "We're not finished. We've barely gotten started."

Crossing into the hall, Will met Raul's questioning stare. "You saw and heard nothing. Are we clear?"

Will waited until the other man silently nodded before walking away. No way in hell did he need his father knowing he'd been caught making out in the damn laundry room with the maid.

Next time, and there would be a next time, Will vowed she'd be in his bed. She was a willing participant every time he'd kissed her. Hell, if the knock hadn't interrupted them, they'd probably both be a lot happier right now.

Regardless of what Cat had just said, he knew full well she wanted him. Her body wasn't lying. What kind of man would he be if he ignored her needs? Because he sure as hell wasn't going to sit back and wait for another man to come along and explore that sexual side.

She was his.

Five

Alma was a beautiful country. Catalina was going to miss the island's beautiful water and white sandy beaches when she left. Swimming was her first love. Being one with the water, letting loose and not caring about anything was the best source of therapy.

And tonight she needed the release.

For three days she'd managed to dodge Will. He had come to Patrick's house every morning, holed himself up in the office with his father and then left, assumedly to head into the Rowling Energy offices.

Will may say he'd changed, but to her he still looked as if he was playing the perfect son, dead set on taking over the family business. Apparently he thought he could take her over as well. But she wasn't a business deal to close and she certainly wouldn't lose her mind again and let him devour her so thoroughly no matter how much she enjoyed it.

Lust was something that would only get her into trouble. The repercussions of lust would last a lifetime; a few moments of pleasure wouldn't be worth the inevitable heartache in the end.

Catalina sliced her arms through the water, cursing herself for allowing thoughts of Will to infringe on her downtime when she only wanted to relax. The man wanted to control her and she was letting him because she had no clue how to stop this emotional roller coaster he'd strapped her into.

Heading toward the shoreline, Catalina pushed herself the last few feet until she could stand. Shoving her short hair back from her face, she took deep breaths as she sloshed through the water. With the sun starting to sink behind her, she crossed the sand and scooped up her towel to mop her face.

He'd seriously crossed the line when he'd asked about her virginity. Yes, she'd gotten carried away with him, even if she did enjoy those stolen moments, but her sexual past was none of his concern because she had no intention of letting him have any more power over her. And she sure as hell didn't want to know about all of his trysts since they'd been together.

Cat wrapped the towel around her body and tucked the edge in to secure the cloth in place. This small stretch of beach wasn't far from her apartment, only a five-minute walk, and rarely had many visitors in the evening. Most people came during the day or on weekends. On occasion, Catalina would see families playing together. Her heart would always seize up a bit then. She longed for the day when she could have a family of her own, but for now, she had her sights set on fashion.

Giving up one dream for another wasn't an option. Who said she couldn't have it all? She could have her ideal career and then her family. She was still young. At twenty-four some women were already married and had children, but she wasn't like most women.

And if Will Rowling thought he could deter her from going after what she wanted, he was delusional. And sexy. Mercy, was the man ever sexy.

No, no, no.

Will and his sexiness had no room in her life, especially her bed, which he'd work his way into if she wasn't on guard constantly.

Catalina pulled out her tank-style sundress and exchanged the towel for the modest coverup. After shoving the towel into her bag, she slid into her sandals and started her walk home. The soft ocean breeze always made her smile. Wherever she moved, she was going to need to be close to water or at least close enough that she could make weekend trips.

This was the only form of exercise she enjoyed, and being so short, every pound really showed. Not that she worried about her weight, but she wanted to feel good about herself and she felt her best when she'd been swimming and her muscles were burning from the strain. She wanted to be able to throw on anything in her closet and have confidence. For her, confidence came with a healthy body.

Catalina crossed the street to her apartment building and smiled at a little girl clutching her mother's hand. Once she reached the stoop leading up to her flat, she dug into her bag for her keys. A movement from the corner of her eye caught her attention. She knew who was there before she fully turned, though.

"What are you doing here, Will?"

She didn't look over her shoulder, but she knew he

followed her. Arguing that he wasn't invited was a moot point; the man did whatever he wanted anyway.

"I came to see you."

When she got to the second floor, she stopped outside her door and slid her key into the lock. "I figured you'd given up."

His rich laughter washed over her chilled skin. Between the warm water and the breezy air, she was going to have to get some clothes on to get warm.

"When have you known me to give up?" he asked.

Throwing a glance over her shoulder, she raised a brow. "Four years ago. You chose your career over a relationship. Seeing me was the big mistake. Ring any bells?"

Will's bright aqua-blue eyes narrowed. "I didn't give up. I'm here now, aren't I?"

"Oh, so I was just put on hold until you were ready," she mocked. "How silly of me not to realize."

"Can I come in?" he asked. "I promise I'll only be a couple minutes."

"You can do a lot of damage in a couple minutes," she muttered, but figured the sooner she let him in, the sooner he'd leave…she hoped.

Catalina pushed the door open and started toward her bedroom. Thankfully the door to the spare room was closed. The last thing she needed was for Will to see everything she'd been working on. Her personal life was none of his concern.

"I'm changing and you're staying out here."

She slammed her bedroom door, hoping he'd get the hint he wasn't welcome. What was he doing here? Did he think she'd love how he came to her turf? Did he think she'd be more comfortable and melt into a puddle at his feet, and then invite him into her bed?

Oh, that man was infuriating. Catalina jerked off

her wet clothes and draped them over her shower rod in her bathroom. Quickly she threw on a bra, panties and another sundress, one of her own designs she liked to wear out. It was simple, but it was hers, and her confidence was always lifted when she wore her own pieces.

Her damp hair wasn't an issue right now. All she wanted to know was why he was here. If he only came for another make-out scene that was going to leave her frustrated and angry, she wanted no part of it. She smoothed back a headband to keep her hair from her face. It was so short it would be air-dried in less than an hour.

Padding barefoot back into her living room, she found Will standing near the door where she'd left him. He held a small package in his hands that she hadn't noticed before. Granted she'd had her back to him most of the time because she didn't want to face him.

"Come bearing gifts?" she asked. "Didn't you learn your lesson after the flowers?"

Will's smile spread across his face. "Thought I'd try a different tactic."

On a sigh, Catalina crossed the room and sank into her favorite cushy chair. "Why try at all? Honestly. Is this just a game to see if you can get the one who got away? Are you trying to prove to yourself that you can conquer me? Is it a slumming thing? What is it, Will? I'm trying to understand this."

He set the box on the coffee table next to a stack of the latest fashion magazines. After taking a seat on her couch, Will rested his elbows on his knees and leaned forward.

Silence enveloped them and the longer he sat there, the more Catalina wondered what was going through his mind. Was he planning on lying? Was he trying to figure out how to tell her the truth? Or perhaps he was second-guessing himself.

She studied him—his strong jawline, his broad frame taking up so much space in her tiny apartment. She'd never brought a man here. Not that she'd purposely brought Will here, but having such a powerful man in her living room was a new experience for her.

Maybe she was out of her league. Maybe she couldn't fight a force like Will Rowling. But she was sure as hell going to try because she couldn't stand to have her heart crushed so easily again.

Catalina curled her feet beside her in the spacious chair as Will met her gaze. Those piercing aqua eyes forced her to go still.

"What if I'm here because I've never gotten over you?"

Dammit. Why did he let that out? He wasn't here to make some grand declaration. He was here to soften her, to get her to let down that guard a little more because he was not giving up. He'd jump through whatever hoop she threw in front of him, but Cat would be his for a while. A steamy affair that no one knew about was exactly what they needed whether she wanted to admit it or not.

When he'd been given the ultimatum by his father to give up Cat or lose his place in Rowling Energy, Will hadn't had much choice. Oh, and his father had also stated that he'd make sure Catalina Iberra would never work anywhere in Alma again if Will didn't let her go.

He'd had to protect her, even though she hated him at the time. He'd do it all over again. But he didn't want to tell her what had happened. He didn't want her to feel guilty or to pity him. Will would win her back just as he'd won her the first time. He'd be charming and wouldn't take no for an answer.

His quiet, almost vulnerable question still hung heavy in the space between them as he waited for her response. She hadn't kicked him out of her flat, so he was making progress. Granted, he'd been making progress since that spur-of-the-moment kiss a month ago, but he'd rather speed things along. A man only had so much control over his emotions.

"You can have any woman you want." Catalina toyed with the edge of the hem on her dress, not making eye contact. "You let me go, you called me a mistake."

He'd regret those words until he died. To know he'd made Cat feel less than valuable to him was not what he'd wanted to leave her with, but once the damning words were out, he couldn't take them back. Anything he said after that point would have been moot. The damage had been done and he'd moved on...or tried to. He'd said hurtful things to get her to back away from him; he'd needed her to stay away at the time because he couldn't afford to let her in, not when his father had such a heavy hand.

Will had been devastated when she'd started dating another man. What had he expected? Did he think a beautiful, vibrant woman was just going to sit at home and sulk about being single? Obviously she had taken the breakup better than he had. And how sick was that, that he wished she'd been more upset? He wanted her to be happy...he just wanted it to be with him.

"I can't have any woman," he countered. "You're still avoiding me."

She lifted her dark eyes, framed by even darker lashes, and focused on him. Every time she looked at him, Will felt that punch to the gut. Lust. It had to be lust because he wouldn't even contemplate anything else. They'd been apart too long for any other emotion to have settled in. They were two different people now and he just wanted to get to know her all over again, to prove himself to her. She deserved everything he had to give.

Will came to his feet. He couldn't stay here because the longer he was around her, the more he wanted her. Cat was going to be a tough opponent and he knew all too well that the best things came from patience and outlasting your opponent. Hadn't it taken him four years to best his father? And he was still in the process of doing that.

"Where are you going?" she asked, looking up at him.

"You want me to stay?" He stepped forward, easing closer to the chair she sat in. "Because if I stay, I'm going to want more than just talking."

"Did you just come to see where I lived? Did you need this reminder of how opposite we are? How I'm just—"

Will put his hand over her mouth. Leaning down, he gripped the arm of her chair and rested his weight there. He eased in closer until he could see the black rim around her dark eyes.

"We've been over this. I don't care what you are. I know what I want, what I need, and that's you."

Her eyes remained locked on his. Slowly he drew his hand away and trailed his fingertips along the thin tan line coming down from behind her neck.

"You're getting red here," he murmured, watching her shiver beneath his touch. "I haven't seen you out of work clothes in years. You need to take better care of your skin."

Cat reached up, grabbed his hand and halted his movements. "Don't do this, Will. There's nothing for you here and I have nothing to give. Even if I gave you my body, I'd regret it because you wouldn't give me any more and I deserve so much. I see that now and I won't lose sight of my goals just because we have amazing chemistry."

Her pleading tone had him easing back. She wanted him. He'd broken her down enough for her to fully admit it.

What goals was she referring to? He wanted to know what her plans were because he wouldn't let this go. He'd waited too long for this second chance and to finally have her, to finally show his father he was in control now, was his ultimate goal.

"I'm not about to give up, Cat." Will stood straight up and kept his eyes on hers. "You have your goals, I have mine."

As he turned and started walking toward the door, he glanced back and nodded toward the package on the table. "You didn't like flowers. This may be more practical for you."

Before she could say a word, he let himself out. Leaving her flat was one of the hardest things he'd done. He knew if he'd hung around a bit longer she would give in to his advances, but he wanted her to come to him. He wanted her to be aching for him, not reluctant.

Cat would come around. They had too much of a history and a physical connection now for her to ignore her body. He had plenty to keep him occupied until she decided to come to him.

Starting with dropping another bomb on his father where their investments and loyalties lay.

Six

Damn that man.

Catalina resisted the urge to march into the Rowling Energy offices and throw Will's gift back in his face.

But she'd used the thing all weekend. Now she was back at the Playa del Onda estate cleaning for his father. Same old thing, different day.

Still, the fact that Will had brought her a sewing kit, a really nice, really expensive sewing kit, had her smiling. She didn't want to smile at his gestures. She wanted to be grouchy and hate them. The flowers had been easy to cast aside, but something as personal as the sewing kit was much harder to ignore.

Will had no idea about her love of sewing, he'd merely gotten the present because of the shirt she'd ripped the other day. Even though he had no clue of her true passion, he thought outside the proverbial box and took the time to find something to catch her attention… as if he hadn't been on her radar already.

Catalina shoved a curtain rod through the grommets and slid it back into place on the hook. She'd long put off laundering the curtains in the glass-enclosed patio room. She'd been too distracted since that initial kiss nearly a month ago.

Why, after four years, why did Will have to reawaken those feelings? Why did he have to be so bold, so powerful, making her face those desires that had never fully disappeared?

The cell in her pocket vibrated. Pulling the phone out, she glanced down to see Patrick's name on the screen. She wasn't afraid of her boss, but she never liked getting a call from him. Either she'd done something wrong or he was about to unload a project on her. He'd been so much more demanding than James had. Granted James had traveled all over the world for football and had rarely been home, but even when he was, he treated Catalina with respect.

Patrick acted as if the dirt on his shoe had a higher position in the social order than she did.

But she needed every dime she could save so that she could leave once she'd finished all her designs. She made a good income for a maid, but she had no idea how much she'd need to start over in a new country and get by until she got her big break.

"Hello?" she answered.

"Come to my office."

She stared at the phone as he hung up. So demanding, so controlling…much like his son.

Catalina made her way through the house and down the wide hall toward Patrick's office. Was Will here today? She didn't want to pry or ask, but she had a feeling Patrick was handing over the reins to the twin he'd groomed for the position.

The office door stood slightly ajar, so Catalina tapped her knuckles against the thick wood before entering.

"Sir," she said, coming to stand in front of Patrick's wide mahogany desk.

The floral arrangement she'd brought a few days ago still sat on the edge. Catalina had to suppress her grin at the fact that the gift a billionaire purchased for a maid now sat on said billionaire's father's desk.

When Patrick glanced up at her, she swallowed. Why did he always make her feel as if she was in the principal's office? She'd done nothing wrong and had no reason to worry.

Oh, wait. She'd made out with his son in the laundry room and there had been a witness outside the door. There was that minor hiccup in her performance.

"I'm going to have the Montoro family over for a dinner," Patrick stated without preamble. "With the passing of Isabella, it's fitting we extend our condolences and reach out to them during this difficult time."

Catalina nodded. "Of course. Tell me what we need."

"The funeral will be Wednesday and I know they will have their own gathering. I'd like to have the dinner Friday night."

Catalina pulled out her cell and started typing in the notes as he rattled off the details. Only the Montoros and the Rowlings would be in attendance. Patrick expected her to work that day preparing the house and that evening cleaning up after the party… Long days like that were a killer for her back and feet. But the double time pay more than made up for the aches and pains.

"Is that all?" she asked when he stopped talking.

He nodded. "There is one more thing."

Catalina swallowed, slid her phone into her pocket and clasped her hands in front of her body. "Yes, sir?"

"If you have a notion of vying for my son's attention, it's best you stop." Patrick eased back in his chair as if he had all the power and not a worry in the world. "He may not be marrying Bella as I'd hoped, but that doesn't mean he's on the market for you. Will is a billionaire. He's handling multimillion dollar deals on a daily basis and the last thing he has time for is to get tangled up in the charms of my maid."

The threat hung between them. Patrick wasn't stupid; he knew exactly what was going on with his own son. Catalina wasn't going to be a pawn in their little family feud. She had a job to do. She'd do it and be on her way in just a few months. Patrick and Will would still be bringing in money and she'd be long forgotten.

"I have no claim on your son, Mr. Rowling," she stated, thankful her voice was calm and not shaky. "I apologize if you think I do. We dated years ago but that's over."

Patrick nodded. "Let's make sure it stays that way. You have a place here and it's not in Will's life."

Even though he spoke the truth, a piece of her heart cracked a bit more over the fact.

"I'll get to work on these arrangements right away," she told Patrick, purposely dropping the topic of his son.

Catalina escaped the office, making it out to the hall before she leaned back against the wall and closed her eyes. Deep breaths in and out. She forced herself to remain calm.

If Patrick had known what happened in the laundry room days ago, he would've outright said so. He wasn't a man known for mincing words. But he knew something was up, which was all the more reason for her to stay clear of Will and his potent touch, his hypnotizing kisses and his spellbinding aqua eyes.

Pushing off the wall, Catalina made her way to the kitchen to speak to the head chef. They had a dinner to discuss and Catalina needed to focus on work, not the man who had the ability to destroy her heart for a second time.

He'd watched her bustle around for the past hour. She moved like a woman on a mission and she hadn't given him one passing glance.

Will wouldn't tolerate being ignored, especially by a woman he was so wrapped up in.

Slipping from the open living area where Cat was rearranging seating and helping the florist with new arrangements, Will snuck into the hallway and pulled his phone from his pocket. Shooting off a quick text, he stood in a doorway to the library and waited for a reply.

And waited. And waited.

Finally after nearly ten minutes, his phone vibrated in his hand. Cat hadn't dismissed him completely, but she wasn't accepting his offer of a private talk. What the hell? She was just outright saying no?

Unacceptable.

He sent another message.

Meet me once the guests arrive. You'll have a few minutes to spare once you're done setting up.

Will read over his message and quickly typed another. I'll be in the library.

Since he hadn't seen his father yet, Will shot his dad a message stating he may be a few minutes late. There was no way he could let another opportunity pass him by to be alone with Cat.

He'd worked like a madman these past few days and

hadn't even had a chance to stop by for a brief glimpse of her. He knew his desires ran deep, but he hadn't realized how deep until he had to go this long without seeing her, touching her, kissing her.

In the past two days Will had severed longstanding ties with another company that wasn't producing the results he wanted. Again he'd faced the wrath of his father, but yet again, Will didn't care. This was his time to reign over Rowling Energy and he was doing so by pushing forward, hard and fast. He wasn't tied to these companies the way his father was and Will intended to see the real estate division double its revenues in the next year.

But right now, he didn't want to think about finances, investments, real estate or oil. He wanted to focus on how fast he could get Cat in his arms once she entered the room. His body responded to the thought.

She wasn't even in the same room and he was aching for her.

Will had plans for the weekend, plans that involved her. He wanted to take her away somewhere she wouldn't expect, somewhere they could be alone and stop tiptoeing around the chemistry. Stolen kisses here and there were getting old. He felt like a horny teenager sneaking around his father's house copping a feel of his girl.

Will took a seat on the leather sofa near the floor-to-ceiling windows. He kept the lights off, save for a small lamp on the table near the entryway. That soft glow was enough; he didn't want to alert anyone who might be wandering outside that there was a rendezvous going on in here.

Finally after he felt as if he'd waited for an hour,

the door clicked softly and Cat appeared. She shut the door at her back, but didn't step farther into the room.

"I don't have much time," she told him.

He didn't need much…yet. Right now all he needed was one touch, just something to last until he could execute his weekend plans.

Will stood and crossed the spacious room, keeping his eyes locked on hers the entire time. With her back to the door, he placed a hand on either side of her face and leaned in.

His lips grazed over hers softly. "I've missed kissing you."

Cat's body trembled. When her hands came up to his chest, he thought she'd take the initiative and kiss him, but she pushed him away.

"I know I've given mixed signals," she whispered. "But this has to end. No matter how much I enjoy kissing you, no matter how I want you, I don't have the energy for this and I can't lose my j—"

Cat put a hand over her mouth, shook her head and glanced away.

"Your job?" he asked, taking hold of her wrist and prying her hand from her lips. "You think you're going to lose your job over what we have going?"

Her deep eyes jerked back to his. "We have nothing going, Will. Don't you get that? You can afford to mess around. You have nothing at stake here."

He had more than she realized.

"I need to get back to the guests. Bella and James just arrived."

He gripped her elbow before she could turn from him. "Stop. Give me two minutes."

Tucking her hair behind her ears, she nodded. "No more."

Will slid his thumb beneath her eyes. "You're exhausted. I don't like you working so hard, Cat."

"Some of us don't have a choice."

If she were his woman, she'd never work a day in her life.

Wait. What was he saying? She wasn't his woman and he wasn't looking to make her his lifelong partner, either. Marriage or any type of committed relationship was sure as hell not something he was ready to get into. Yes, he wanted her and wanted to spend time with her, but anything beyond that wasn't on his radar just yet.

Gliding his hands over her shoulders, he started to massage the tense muscles. His thumbs grazed the sides of her neck. Cat let out a soft moan as she let her head fall back against the door.

"What are you doing to me?" she groaned.

"Giving you the break you've needed."

Will couldn't tear his gaze from her parted lips, couldn't stop himself from fantasizing how she would look when he made love to her…when, not if.

"I really need to get back." Cat lifted her head and her lids fluttered open. "But this feels so good."

Will kept massaging. "I want to make you feel better," he muttered against her lips. "Let me take you home tonight, Cat."

On a sigh, she shook her head and reached up to squeeze his hands, halting his movements. "You have to know your father thinks something is going on with us."

Will stilled. "Did he say something to you?"

Her eyes darted away. "It doesn't matter. What matters is I'm a maid. You're a billionaire ready to take on the world. We have different goals, Will."

Yeah, and the object of his main goal was plastered against his body.

Will gripped her face between his palms and forced her to look straight at him. "What did he say?"

"I'm just fully aware of my role in this family and it's not as your mistress."

Fury bubbled through Will. "Patrick Rowling does not dictate my sex life and he sure as hell doesn't have a clue what's going on with us."

The sheen in her eyes only made Will that much angrier. How dare his father say anything? He'd done that years ago when Will had let him steamroll over his happiness before. Not again.

"There's nothing going on between us," she whispered.

Will lightened his touch, stroked her bottom lip with the pads of his thumbs. "Not yet, but there will be."

Capturing her lips beneath his, Will relaxed when Cat sighed into his mouth. Will pulled back because if he kept kissing her, he was going to want more and he'd be damned if he had Cat for the first time in his father's library.

When he took Cat to bed, it would be nowhere near Patrick Rowling or his house.

"Get back to work," he muttered against her lips. "We'll talk later."

"Will—"

"Later," he promised with another kiss. "I'm not done with you, Cat. I told you once, I've barely started."

He released her and let her leave while he stayed behind.

If he walked out now, people would know he'd been hiding with Cat. The last thing he ever intended was to get her in trouble or risk her job. He knew she took pride in what she did and the fact she was a perfectionist only made Will respect her more. She was so much more, though. She was loyal and determined. Qualities he admired.

Well, he was just as determined and his father would never interfere with his personal life again. They'd gone that round once before and Patrick had won. This time, Will intended to come out, not only on top, but with Rowling Energy and Cat both belonging to him.

Seven

Will stared over the rim of his tumbler as he sipped his scotch. The way Cat worked the room was something he'd seen in the past, but he hadn't fully appreciated the charm she portrayed toward others during such a difficult time.

There were moments where she'd been stealthy as she slipped in and out of the room, removing empty glasses and keeping the hors d'oeuvre trays filled. Will was positive others hadn't even noticed her, but he did. He noticed every single thing about her.

The dinner was due to be served in thirty minutes and the guests had mostly arrived. Bella stood off to the side with her brother Gabriel, his arm wrapped around her shoulders.

"Your maid is going to get a complex if you keep drilling holes into her."

Will stiffened at James's words. His brother came to stand beside him, holding his own tumbler of scotch.

"I'm not drilling holes," Will replied, tossing back the last of his drink. He welcomed the burn and turned to set the glass on the accent table. "I'm making sure she's okay."

James's brief laugh had Will gritting his teeth to remain quiet and to prevent himself from spewing more defensive reasons as to why he'd been staring at Cat.

"She's used to working, Will. I'd say she's just fine."

Will turned to face his twin. "Did you come over here to hassle me or did you actually want to say something important?"

James's smile spread across his face. Will knew that smile, dammit. He'd thrown it James's way when he'd been in knots over Bella.

"Shut up," Will said as he turned back to watch Cat.

If his brother already had that knowing grin, then Will's watching Cat wouldn't matter at this point. She was working too damn hard. She'd been here all day to make sure the house was perfect for the Montoros and she was still busting her butt to make everyone happy. The chef was really busting it, too, behind the scenes. Cat was definitely due for a much needed relaxing day away from all of this.

"You appear to be plotting," James commented. "But right now I want to discuss what Dad is in such a mood about."

Will threw his brother a glance. "He's Patrick Rowling. Does he need a reason?"

"Not necessarily, but he was a bit gruffer than usual when I spoke with him earlier."

Will watched his father across the room as the man approached Bella and Gabriel. As they all spoke, Will knew his father was diplomatic enough to put on a front of being compassionate. He wouldn't be his stiff, grouchy self with those two.

"I may have made some business decisions he wasn't happy with," Will stated simply.

"Business? Yeah, that will do it." James sighed and finished his scotch. "He put you in charge, so he can't expect you to run every decision by him."

"That's what I told him. I'm not one of his employees, I'm his son and I'm the CEO of Rowling Energy now."

"Plus you're trying to seduce his maid," James added with a chuckle. "You're going to get grounded."

Will couldn't help but smile. "You're such an ass."

"It's fun to see the tables turned and you squirming over a woman for once."

"I'm not squirming, dammit," Will muttered.

But he wouldn't deny he was using Cat as another jab at his father. Yes, he wanted Cat and always had, but if being with her still irritated the old man, so much the better.

Part of him felt guilty for the lack of respect for his father, but that went both ways and the moment Patrick had issued his ultimatum years ago, Will had vowed then and there to gain back everything he deserved, no matter what the cost to his relationship with his father.

Bella's oldest brother, Rafe, and his very pregnant wife, Emily, crossed the room, heading for Will and James. Since he'd abdicated, Rafe and Emily had lived in Key West. But they'd traveled back to be with the family during this difficult time.

"This was a really nice thing for Patrick to do," Rafe stated as he wrapped an arm around his wife's waist. "Losing Isabella has been hard."

"I'm sorry for your loss," Will said. "She was definitely a fighter and Alma is a better place because of her."

"She was quite stubborn," Emily chimed in with a smile. "But we'll get through this because the Montoros are strong."

Will didn't think this was the appropriate time to bring up the subject of Rafe resigning from his duties before his coronation. It was the proverbial elephant in the room.

"I'm going to save my wife from my father," James told them. "Excuse me."

Rafe and Emily were talking about the funeral— how many people had turned out and how supportive the country was in respecting their time of mourning. But Will was only half listening. Cat glanced his way once and that's all it took for his heart to kick up and his body to respond. She didn't smile, she merely locked those dark eyes on him as if she knew his every thought.

Tension crackled between them and everyone else in the room disappeared from his world. Nobody existed but Cat and he knew without a doubt she would agree to his proposal.

He wouldn't accept no for an answer.

Her feet were absolutely screaming. Her back wasn't faring much better. The Montoros lingered longer than she'd expected and Catalina had stuck around an hour after the guests had left.

This fourteen-hour workday would certainly yield a nice chunk of change, but right now all Catalina could think of was her bed, which she hoped to fall into the moment she got home. She may not even take the time to peel out of her clothes.

Catalina nearly wept as she walked toward her car.

She'd parked in the back of the estate near the detached garage where Patrick kept his sporty cars that he only brought out on special occasions. The motion light popped on as she approached her vehicle.

Instantly she spotted Will sitting on a decorative bench along the garage wall. Catalina stopped and couldn't help but smile.

"Are you hiding?" she asked as she started forward again.

"Waiting." He unfolded that tall, broad frame and started coming toward her. "I know you're exhausted, but I just wanted to ask something."

Catalina crossed her arms and stared up at him. "You could've called or texted me your question."

"I could've," he agreed with a slight nod. "But you could say no too easily. I figure if you're looking me in the eye—"

"You think I can't resist you?" she laughed.

Exhaustion might have been consuming her and clouding her judgment, but there was still something so irresistible and charming about this overbearing man…and something calculating as well. He'd purposely waited for her, to catch her at a weak moment. He must really want something major.

"I'm hoping." He reached out, tucking her hair behind her ears before his fingertips trailed down her jawline. "I want to take you somewhere tomorrow afternoon. Just us, on my yacht for a day out."

Catalina wanted to give in to him, she wanted to forget all the reasons they shouldn't be together in any way. She wished her head and her heart would get on the same page where Will Rowling was concerned. She had goals, she had a job she needed to keep in order to reach those goals…yet everything about Will made her want to entertain the idea of letting him in, even if just for one night.

"I even have the perfect spot chosen for a swim," he added, resting his hands on her shoulders. Squeezing her tense muscles, Will smiled. "I'll be a total gentleman."

"A total gentleman?" Catalina couldn't help but laugh. "Then why are you so eager to go?"

"Maybe I think it's time someone gives back to you." His hands stilled as he held her gaze and she realized he wasn't joking at all. "And maybe it's time you see that I'm a changed man."

Her heart tumbled in her chest. "I'm so tired, Will. I'm pretty sure I'm going to spend the next two days sleeping."

"You won't have to do a thing," he promised. "I'll bring the food. All you have to do is wear a swimsuit. I promise this will be a day of total relaxation and pampering."

Catalina sighed. "Will, your father—"

"He's not invited."

She laughed again. "I'm serious."

"I am, too."

Will backed her up to her car and towered over her with such an intense gaze, Catalina knew she was fighting a losing battle.

"This has nothing to do with my father, your job or our differences." His strong jaw set firm, he pressed his gloriously hard body against hers as he stared into her eyes. "I want to spend time with you, Cat. I've finally got my sights set on what is important to me and I'm not letting you get away again. Not without a fight."

"That's what scares me." She whispered the confession.

"There's nothing to be afraid of."

"Said the big bad wolf."

Will smiled, dropped his hands and eased back. "No pressure, Cat. I want to spend time with you, but if you're not ready, I understand. I'm not going anywhere."

The man knew exactly what to say and his delivery was flawless. In his line of work, Will was a master at getting people to see things his way, to ensure he got what he wanted at the end of the day.

No matter what common sense tried to tell her, Catalina wasn't about to start in on a battle she had no chance of winning.

"I'll go," she told him.

The smile that spread across his face was half shadowed by the slant of the motion lights, but she knew all too well how beautiful and sexy the gesture was.

"I'll pick you up at your apartment around noon," he told her. "Now, go home. I'm going to follow you to make sure you get there safely since you're so tired."

"That's not necessary."

Will shrugged. "Maybe not, but I wasn't kidding when I said someone needed to take care of you and pamper you for a change. I'm not coming in. I'll just follow, and then be on my way home."

"I live in the opposite direction from your house," she argued.

"We could've been halfway to your flat by now." He slid his arm around her and tugged on her door handle. "Get in, stop fighting me and let's just save time. You know I'll win in the end anyway."

That's precisely what she feared the most. Will having a win over her could prove more damaging than the last time she'd let him in, but she wanted to see this new side of him. She wanted to take a day and do absolutely nothing but be catered to.

Catalina eased behind the wheel and let Will shut her door. Tomorrow would tell her one of two things: either she was ready to move on and just be his friend or she wanted more with him than stolen kisses behind closed doors.

Worry and panic flooded Catalina as she realized she already knew what tomorrow would bring.

Will had been meaning to see his niece, Maisey, and this morning he was making her his top priority. Before he went to pick up Cat for their outing, he wanted to surprise his adorable niece with a gift…the first of many. He had a feeling this little girl was going to be spoiled, which was better than a child being ignored.

Maisey Rowling would want for nothing. Will's brother had given up being a playboy and was growing into his family-man role rather nicely, and Bella was the perfect stepmother to the infant. Will figured since he and his twin were growing closer, he'd stop in and offer support to James. This complete one-eighty in lifestyles had to be a rough transition for James, but he had Bella and the two were completely in love. And they both loved sweet Maisey.

A slight twinge of jealousy speared through Will, but not over the fact that his brother had married Bella. There had been no chemistry between Will and Bella. She was sweet and stunning, but Will only had eyes for one woman.

The jealousy stemmed from the thought of his brother settling down with his own family. Will hadn't given much thought to family before. He'd been raised to focus solely on taking over Rowling Energy one day.

Will tapped on the etched glass front door to James and Bella's temporary home. They were living here until they knew for sure where they wanted to be permanently. They were in the middle of renovating the old farmhouse that belonged to the Montoros and James had mentioned that they'd probably end up there.

But for now, this house was ideal. It was near the beach, near the park and near Bella's family. Family was important to the Montoros…and yet Will was still thrilled he'd dodged that clan.

The door swung open and Bella greeted him with a smile. "Will, this is a surprise. Come on in."

Clutching the doll he'd brought as a present, Will stepped over the threshold. "I should've called, but I really thought of this last-minute."

Bella smoothed her blond hair behind her shoulders. "This is fine. Maisey and James are in the living room. They just finished breakfast and they're watching a movie."

Her blue eyes darted down to his hands. "I'm assuming that's for Maisey?"

Will nodded. "I haven't played the good uncle yet. Figured it was time I started spoiling her."

Bella's smile lit up her face. "She's going to love it."

The thought of being married to this woman did nothing for Will. Yes, she was stunning, but he'd never felt the stirrings of lust or need when he'd been around her. Their fathers never should have attempted to arrange their engagement, but thankfully everything had worked out for the best…at least where Bella and James were concerned. They were a unified family now.

The thought of his black sheep, playboy brother snuggling up with a baby girl and watching some kid flick was nearly laughable. But Will also knew that once James had learned he had a child, his entire life had changed and his priorities had taken on a whole new order, Maisey being at the top.

Bella led Will through a wide, open-arched doorway to a spacious living room. Two pale yellow sofas sat facing each other with a squat, oversized table between them. An array of coloring books and crayons were scattered over the top of the glossy surface.

James sat on one of the sofas, legs sprawled out before him with Maisey on his lap. James's short hair was all in disarray. He still wore his pajama bottoms and no shirt, and Maisey had a little pink nightgown on; it was obvious they were enjoying a morning of laziness.

As Will stepped farther into the room, James glanced over and smiled. "Hey, brother. What brings you out?"

Bella sat at the end of the couch at her husband's feet. Maisey crawled over her father's legs and settled herself onto Bella's lap. Will looked at his niece and found himself staring into those signature Rowling aqua eyes. No denying who this baby's father was.

"I brought something for Maisey." Will crossed the room and sat on the edge of the coffee table. "Hey, sweetheart. Do you like dolls?"

What if she didn't like it? What if she didn't like him? Dammit. He should've planned better and called to see what Maisey actually played with. He'd just assumed a little girl would like a tiny stuffed doll.

"Her dress matches your nightgown," Bella said softly to the little girl.

Maisey kept her eyes on him as she reached for the toy. Instantly the blond hair went into Maisey's mouth.

"She likes it." James laughed. "Everything goes into her mouth these days."

Will continued to stare at his niece. Children were

one area where he had no clue, but if James said Maisey liked it, then Will had to assume she did.

James swung his legs to the floor and leaned forward. "You hungry?" he asked. "We still have some pancakes and bacon in the kitchen."

"No, I'm good. I'm getting ready to pick up Cat, so I can't stay anyway."

James's brows lifted as he shot Bella a look. "Is this a date?"

Will hadn't intended on telling anyone, but in growing closer with James over the past couple months, he realized he wanted this bond with his twin. Besides, after their conversation last night, James pretty much knew exactly where Will stood in regards to Cat.

He trusted James, that had never been an issue. The issue they'd had wedged between them stemmed from their father always doting on one brother, molding him into a disciple, while ostracizing the other one.

"I'm taking her out on my yacht," Will told him. "We're headed to one of the islands for the day. I'm hoping for total seclusion. Most tourists don't know about them."

There was a small cluster of islands off the coast of Alma. He planned on taking her to Isla de Descanso. The island's name literally meant Island of Relaxation. Cat deserved to be properly pampered and he was going to be the man to give her all of her needs…every single one.

"Sounds romantic." Bella shifted Maisey on her lap as she stared at Will. "I wasn't aware you and Catalina were getting more serious."

James laughed. "I think they've been sneaking."

"We're not serious and we're not sneaking," Will

defended himself. "Okay, fine. We were sneaking, but she's private and she's still leery of me."

"You can't blame her," James added.

Will nodded. "I don't, which is why we need this time away from everything. Plus she's working like crazy for Dad and she's never appreciated."

James snorted. "He barely appreciates his sons. You think he appreciates a maid? I was worried when he moved into my old house. I tried to warn her, but she said she could handle it and she needed the job."

Will hated the thought of her having to work. Hated how much she pushed herself for little to no praise and recognition.

"Well, I appreciate her," Bella chimed in. "I saw how hard she worked the dinner last night. I can't imagine the prep that she and the cooks went through, plus the cleanup after. Catalina is a dedicated, hard worker."

"She won't stay forever," James stated as he leaned over and ruffled Maisey's hair.

Will sat up straighter. "What do you mean?"

His brother's eyes came back to meet his. "I'm just saying someone who is such a perfectionist and self-disciplined surely has a long-term goal in mind. I can't imagine she'll want to play maid until she's old and gray. She hinted a few times when she worked for me that she hoped to one day leave Alma."

Leave Alma? The thought hadn't even crossed Will's mind. Would Cat really go somewhere else? Surely not. Her mother still worked here. She used to work for Patrick, but years ago she had suddenly quit and gone to work for another prominent family. Cat had been with the Rowlings for five years, but James was right. Someone as vibrant as Cat wouldn't want to dust and wash sheets her entire life. He'd already seen the toll her end-less hours were taking on her.

Will came to his feet, suddenly more eager than ever to see her, to be alone with her. "I better get going. I just wanted to stop by and see Maisey before I headed out."

James stood as well. "I'll walk you to the door."

Bidding a goodbye to Bella and Maisey, Will fol-lowed his brother to the foyer.

"Don't say a word about Cat and me," Will said.

Gripping the doorknob, James nodded. "I'm not say-ing a word. I already know Dad would hate the idea and he's interfered enough in our personal lives lately. And I'm not judging you and Catalina. I actually think you two are a good match."

"Thanks, man, but don't let this happily-ever-after stuff you have going on filter into my world. I'm just spending time with Cat. That's all." Will gave his brother a one-armed man hug. "I'll talk to you next week."

Will headed toward his car, more than ready to pick up Cat and get this afternoon started. He planned to be in complete control, but he'd let her set the tone. As much as he wanted her, he wasn't going to pressure her and he wasn't going to deceive her.

Yes, there was the obvious appeal of the fact that his father would hate Will bedding the maid, but he wouldn't risk her job that way even to get petty revenge on his domineering father.

Besides, Cat was so much more than a romp. He couldn't figure out exactly what she was…and that ir-ritated him.

But now he had another worry. What was Cat's ul-timate goal in life? Would she leave Alma and pursue something more meaningful? And why did he care? He wasn't looking for a ring on his finger and he wasn't about to place one on hers, either.

Still, the fact that she could leave bothered him more than he cared to admit.

Will pushed those thoughts aside. Right now, for today, all he was concerned with was Cat and being alone with her. All other world problems would have to wait.

Eight

Nerves kicked around in Catalina's belly as she boarded the yacht. Which seemed like such a simple word for this pristine, massive floating vessel. The fact that the Rowlings had money was an understatement, but to think that Will could own something this amazing…it boggled her mind. She knew he would make a name for himself, knew he'd climb to the top of Rowling Energy. There was never any doubt which twin Patrick was grooming for the position.

But she wasn't focusing on or even thinking of Patrick today. Will wanted her to relax, wanted her to enjoy her day off, and she was going to take full advantage.

Turning toward Will, Catalina laughed as he stepped on board. "I'm pretty sure my entire flat would fit on this deck."

Near the bow, she surveyed the wide, curved outdoor seating complete with plush white pillows. There was even a hot tub off to the side. Catalina couldn't even imagine soaking in that warm water out under the stars. This yacht screamed money, relaxation…and seduction.

She'd voluntarily walked right into the lion's den.

"Let me show you around." Will took hold of her elbow and led her to the set of steps that went below deck. "The living quarters are even more impressive."

Catalina clutched her bag and stepped down as Will gestured for her to go first. The amount of space in the open floor plan below was shocking. It was even grander than she'd envisioned. A large king-sized bed sat in the distance and faced a wall of curved windows that overlooked the sparkling water. Waking up to a sunrise every morning would be heavenly. Waking up with your lover beside you would simply be the proverbial icing on the cake.

No. She couldn't think of Will as her lover or icing on her cake. She was here for a restful day and nothing else. Nookie could not play a part in this because she had no doubt the second he got her out of her clothes, she'd have no defense against him. She needed to stay on guard.

A deep, glossy mahogany bar with high stools separated the kitchen from a living area. The living area had a mounted flat-screen television and leather chairs that looked wide enough for at least two people.

The glossy fixtures and lighting only added to the perfection of the yacht. It all screamed bachelor and money…perfect for Will Rowling.

"You've done well for yourself," she told him as she placed her tote bag on a barstool. "I'm impressed."

Will's sidelong smile kicked up her heart rate. They hadn't even pulled away from the dock and he was already getting to her. This was going to be a day full of her willpower battling her emotions and she didn't know if she'd have the strength to fight off Will's advances.

Who was she kidding? Catalina already knew that if Will tried anything she would succumb to his charms. She'd known this the moment she'd accepted his invitation. But that didn't mean she'd drop her wall of defenses so easily. He'd seriously hurt her before and if he wanted to show her what a changed man he was now, she was going to make him work for it.

"Did you think I was taking you out in a canoe for the day?"

"I guess I hadn't given much thought to the actual boat," she replied, resting her arm on the smooth, curved edge of the bar. "I was too worried about your actions."

"Worried you'd enjoy them too much?" he asked with a naughty grin.

"More like concerned I'd have to deflate your ego," she countered with a matching smile. "You're not seriously going to start putting the moves on me now, are you?"

Will placed a hand over his heart. "You wound me, Cat. I'm at least going to get this boat on course before I rip your clothes off."

Catalina's breath caught in her throat.

Will turned and mounted the steps to go above deck, and then froze and threw a sexy grin over his shoulder. "Relax, Cat. I won't do anything you don't want."

The playful banter had just taken a turn, a sharp turn that sent shivers racing through her entire body. Was she prepared for sex with this man? That's what everything leading up to this moment boiled down to.

Cat would be lying to herself if she tried to say she

didn't want Will physically. That had been proven each time he'd kissed her recently.

I won't do anything you don't want, he'd said.

And that was precisely what scared her the most.

With the ocean breeze sliding across his face, Will welcomed the spittle of spray, the taste of salt on his lips. He needed to get a damn grip. He hadn't meant to be so teasing with Cat.

Okay, he had, but he hadn't meant for her to get that panicked look on her face. He knew full well she was battling with herself where he was concerned. There wasn't a doubt in his mind she wanted him physically and that was easy to obtain. But there was part of Will that wanted her to see that he wasn't at all the same man he used to be.

She would get to see that side of him today. He intended to do everything for her, to prove to her just how appreciated she was and how valued. Will had fully stocked the yacht when he'd had this idea a couple days ago. He'd known he would take her out at some point, but it wasn't until he saw her working the crowd, with circles under her eyes and a smile on her face at the dinner last night, that he decided to invite her right away.

With all of the recent upheaval in Alma—the Montoro monarchy drama and Isabella's passing, not to mention Will's taking the reins of Rowling Energy—there was just too much life getting in the way of what he wanted. Too many distractions interfering with his main goal…and his goal was to have Cat.

He may be the good son, the twin who was raised to follow the rules and not question authority. But Will wasn't about to make the same mistake with Cat as he had in the past. The moment he'd let her walk away years ago, he'd already started plotting to get her back. Then the whole debacle with Bella had happened and Will knew more than ever that it was time to make his move with Rowling Energy and Cat.

Spending the day together on his yacht, however, was something totally unrelated to everything else that had happened in their past. Today was all about them and nothing or nobody else. Everything that happened with Cat from here on out was going to be her call…he may just silently nudge and steer her in the right direction. Those initial kisses had reignited the spark they'd left burning long ago and he knew without a doubt that she felt just as passionate as he did.

He didn't blame her one bit for being leery. He'd done some major damage before and she wouldn't let him forget it anytime soon. Not that he could. He'd never forget that look on her face when he'd told her they'd been a mistake and then walked away. That moment had played over and over in his mind for the past several years. Knowing he'd purposely hurt Cat wasn't something he was likely to ever forget.

Still, if she ever discovered the truth, would she see that he'd done it for her? He'd best keep that secret to himself and just stay on course with his plan now. At least she was here, she was talking and she was coming around. The last thing Will wanted to do was rehash the past when they could be spending their time concentrating on the here and now.

Will steered the yacht toward the private island not too far from Alma. In just under an hour he'd have Cat on a beach with a picnic. He wondered when the last time was that she'd had someone do something like that for her, but quickly dismissed the thought. If another man had pampered her, Will sure as hell didn't want to know.

Of course, there was no man in her life now. Will was the one kissing her, touching her. She was his for at least today so he needed to make the most of every moment they were alone. He truly hoped the tiny island was deserted. He'd come here a few times to think, to get away from all the pressure and stress. Only once had he run into other people.

Cat stayed below for the duration of the trip. Perhaps she was trying to gather her own thoughts as well. Maybe she was avoiding him because she thought that taking her out to a private island for sex was so cliché, so easy to read into.

But for reasons Will didn't want to admit or even think about, this day was so much more than sex. *Cat* was more than sex. Yes, he wanted her in the fiercest way imaginable, but he also wanted more from her… he just didn't know what.

No, that was wrong. The first thing he wanted was for her to see him in a different light. He wanted her to see the good in him she'd seen when they'd grown up together, when they'd laughed and shared secrets with each other. He wanted her to see that he wasn't the monster who had ripped her heart out and diminished their relationship into ashes with just a few damning words.

Perhaps this outing wasn't just about him proving to her what a changed man he was, but for him to try to figure out what the hell to do next and how far he wanted to take things with her once they got back to reality.

When he finally pulled up to the dock and secured the yacht, he went below deck. He hoped the last forty-five minutes had given Cat enough time to see that he wasn't going to literally jump her. The playful banter had taken a sexual turn, but he wasn't sorry. He was only sorry Cat hadn't come up once to see him. This initial space was probably for the best. After all, today was the first time they'd been fully alone and not sneaking into the bathroom or laundry area of his father's home for a make-out session.

Yeah, his seduction techniques needed a bit of work to say the least. But he'd had four years to get control over just how he wanted to approach things once he finally got his Cat alone. And now he was ready.

As he stepped below, Will braced his hands on the trim overhead and froze on the last step. Cat lay sideways, curled into a ball on his bed. The innocent pose shouldn't have his body responding, but…well, he was a guy and this woman had had him tied in knots for years.

Will had wanted Cat in his bed for too long. All his fantasies involved the bed in his house, but the yacht would do. At this point he sure as hell wasn't going to be picky. He'd waited too damn long for this and he was going to take each moment he could get, no matter the surroundings.

And the fact that she was comfortable enough to rest here spoke volumes for how far they'd come. Just a few weeks ago he'd kissed her as if she was his next breath and she'd run away angry. Though Will was smart enough to know her anger stemmed from arousal.

Passion and hate…there was such a fine line between the two.

Slowly, Will crossed the open area and pulled a small throw from the narrow linen closet. Gently placing the thin blanket over her bare legs and settling it around her waist, Will watched the calm rise and fall of her chest. She was so peaceful, so relaxed and not on her guard.

For the first time in a long time, Will was finally seeing the woman he knew years ago, the woman who was more trusting, less cautious.

Of course, he'd helped shape her into the vigilant person she was today. Had he not made such bad choices when they'd been together the first time, perhaps she wouldn't have to feel so guarded all the time. Perhaps she'd smile more and laugh the way she used to.

Cat shifted, let out a throaty moan and blinked up at Will. Then her eyes widened as she sat straight up.

"Oh my. Was I asleep?"

Will laughed, crossing his arms over his chest. "Or you were playing dead."

Cat smoothed her short hair away from her face and glanced toward the wall of windows. "I was watching the water. I was so tired, so I thought I'd just lie here and enjoy the scenery."

"That was the whole point in having my bed right there. It's a breathtaking view."

When she turned her attention back to him, she gasped. That's right, he hadn't been discussing the water. The view of the woman was much more enticing.

"Why don't you use the restroom to freshen up and change into your suit?" he suggested. "I'll get our lunch set up."

The bright smile spreading across her face had something unfamiliar tugging on his heart. He may not be able to label what was going on between them, but he couldn't afford to be emotional about it.

Dammit. He didn't even know what to feel, how to act anymore. He wanted her, but he wasn't thinking of forever. He wanted now. He needed her to see he was a different man, yet he was more than ready to throw this relationship into his father's face.

Sticking to business would have been best; at least he knew exactly what he was getting into with real estate and oil. With Cat, he had no clue and the fact that she had him so tied in knots without even trying was terrifying.

Once his mission had been clear—to win back Cat to prove he could and to show his father who was in charge. But then, somewhere along the way, Will had shifted into needing Cat to see the true person he'd come to be, the man who still had feelings for her and cared for her on a level even he couldn't understand.

Cat came to her feet and started folding the throw. "I'm sorry I fell asleep on you."

Stepping forward and closing the space between them, Will pulled the blanket from her hands, wadded it up and threw it into the corner. "You aren't cleaning. You aren't folding, dusting, doing dishes. Your only job is to relax. If you want a nap, take a nap. The day is yours. The cleaning is up to me. Got it?"

Her eyes widened as she glanced at the crumpled blanket. "Are you just going to leave that there?"

Will took her chin between his thumb and finger, forcing her to look only at him. "You didn't answer my question."

Her wide, dark eyes drew him in as she merely nodded. "I can't promise, but I'll try."

Unable to help himself, Will smacked a kiss on her lips and pulled back as a grin spread across his face. "Go freshen up and meet me on the top deck."

Will watched as Cat grabbed her bag off the barstool and crossed to the bathroom. Once the door clicked shut, he let out a breath.

He'd sworn nobody would ever control him or hold any power over him again. Yet here was a petite, doe-eyed maid who had more power over him than any business magnate or his father ever could.

Will raked a hand through his hair. He'd promised Cat a day of relaxation and he intended to deliver just that. If she wasn't ready for more, then he'd have to pull all of his self-control to the surface and honor her wishes.

What had he gotten himself into?

Nine

Maybe bringing this particular swimsuit had been a bad idea. When she'd grabbed the two-piece black bikini, Catalina had figured she'd make Will suffer a little. But, by wearing so little and having him so close, she was the one suffering.

Catalina pulled on a simple red wrap dress from her own collection and slipped on her silver flip-flops.

One glance in the mirror and she laughed. The bikini would at least draw attention away from the haggard lines beneath her eyes and the pallor of her skin. Over the past few months, if she wasn't working for James or Patrick, she was working for herself getting her stock ready to showcase when the opportunity presented itself. She believed in being prepared and the moment she saw an opening with any fashion design firm, she was going to be beating down their doors and promoting her unique styles.

Catalina tossed her discarded clothes back into her tote and looked around to make sure she hadn't left anything lying around in the bathroom. Could such a magnificent room be a simple, mundane bathroom?

With the polished silver fixtures, the glass wall shower and sparkling white tile throughout, Catalina had taken a moment to appreciate all the beauty before she'd started changing. The space screamed dominance...male dominance.

Will was pulling out all the stops today. He'd purposely invited her aboard his yacht because he knew that given her love of water she'd never be able to say no. He was right. Anything that got her away from her daily life and into the refreshing ocean was a no-brainer.

Exiting the bathroom, Catalina dropped her bag next to the door and headed up to the top deck. The sun warmed her skin instantly as she turned and spotted Will in a pair of khaki board shorts and a navy shirt he'd left completely unbuttoned. The man wasn't playing fair...which she assumed was his whole plan from the start.

Fine. She had a bikini and boobs. Catalina figured she'd already won this battle before it began. Men were the simplest of creatures.

Will had transformed the seating area into a picnic. A red throw covered the floor, a bucket with ice and wine sat to one side and Will was pulling fruit from a basket.

"Wow. You really know how to set the stage."

He threw her a smile. "Depends on the audience."

"It's just me, so no need to go to all the trouble." She edged around the curving seats and stood just to the side of the blanket. "I'd be happy with a simple salad."

"There is a need to go to all this trouble," he corrected her as he continued to pull more food from the basket. "Have a seat. The strawberries are fresh, the wine is chilled and I have some amazing dishes for us."

Catalina couldn't turn down an invitation like that. She eased down onto the thick blanket and reached for a strawberry. She'd eaten three by the time Will came to sit beside her.

With his back resting against the sofa, he lifted his knee and wrapped his arm around it. "I have a variety of cheese, salmon, baguettes, a tangy salad my chef makes that will make you weep and for dessert…"

He reached over and pulled the silver lid from the dish. "Your favorite."

Catalina gasped as she stared at the pineapple upside-down cheesecake. "You remembered?"

"Of course I did." He set the lid back down. "There's not a detail about you that I've forgotten, Cat."

When she glanced over at him, she found his eyes locked on hers and a small smile dancing around his lips. "I remembered how much you love strawberries and that you will always pick a fruity dessert over a chocolate one. I also recall how much you love salmon, so I tried to incorporate all of your favorites into this lunch."

Strawberry in hand, she froze. "But you just asked me last night. How did you get all of this together?"

Will shrugged and made up a plate for her. "I knew I wanted to take you out on my yacht at some point. I was hoping for soon, but it wasn't until yesterday that I realized how hard you've been working."

He passed her the plate with a napkin. "You need this break and I want to be the one to give it to you. Besides, there's a lot I can do with a few hours and the right connections."

Catalina smiled as she picked up a cube of cheese.

"I'm sure your chef was making the cheesecake before the crack of dawn this morning."

Will shrugged. "Maybe. He did have nearly everything else done by the time I headed out to James and Bella's house this morning."

"You visited James already, too?"

Will settled back with his own plate and forked up a bite of salmon before answering. "I wanted to see Maisey before James heads back out on the road for football. I haven't really bonded with her much, especially with the strain on my relationship with James. But we're getting there and I wanted to see my niece. I'm sure she and Bella will accompany James on the road when they can."

Something inside Catalina warmed at the image of Will playing the doting, spoiling uncle. A family was definitely in her future plans, but knowing Will was taking an active part in little Maisey's life awakened something in her she hadn't yet uncovered.

But no. Will couldn't be father material. He wasn't even husband material. No matter how much, at one time, she'd wished he was. Will was a career-minded, power-driven man who valued family, but he didn't scream minivan and family portraits.

"How did the bonding go?" she asked, trying to concentrate on her food and not the fact that the image had been placed in her head of Will with a baby. Was there anything sexier than a big, powerful man holding an innocent child?

"She seemed to like the doll I brought her."

Of course he'd brought a doll. Now his "aww" level just exploded. Why did the man have to be so appealing on every single level? She didn't want to find him even more irresistible. She couldn't afford to let her heart get tangled up with him again.

Catalina couldn't handle the struggle within her. "You took her a doll? Did your assistant or someone on your staff go buy it?"

Will glanced at her, brows drawn in. "No, I bought it the other day when I was out and just got the chance to take it to her this morning. Why?"

The man was gaining ground and scaling that wall of defenses she'd so carefully erected. And in unexpected ways. He'd wanted to have a special moment with his niece, which had nothing to do with Catalina. Yet here she sat, on his boat, eating her favorite foods that he'd remembered while listening to him talk of his love for his baby niece.

Why was she keeping him at a distance again?

Oh, yeah. That broken heart four years ago.

They ate the rest of their lunch in silence, except when she groaned like a starved woman as she inhaled her piece of cheesecake. As promised, Will cleaned up the mess and took everything back down to the galley. Once he returned, he extended his hand to her.

"Ready to go for a walk?" he asked.

Catalina placed her hand in his, allowing him to pull her up. "I'm not sure I can walk after that, but I can waddle. I'm pretty stuffed."

Will laughed as he led her from the boat. Once they stepped off the wooden dock, Catalina slipped out of her sandals to walk on the warm, sandy beach. The sand wasn't too hot to burn her feet and as the soft grains shifted beneath her, she found herself smiling. She couldn't remember the last time she'd done absolutely nothing by way of working in one form or another.

"I hope that smile has something to do with me,"

Will stated, again slipping his hand into hers as they walked along the shoreline.

"I'm just happy today. I needed a break and I guess I didn't realize it."

"From one workaholic to another, I recognized the signs."

His confession had her focusing on the words and not how powerful and wonderful his fingers felt laced with hers.

"I never thought you took a break," she replied.

Catalina looked at all the tiny seashells lining the shore and made a mental note to find some beautiful ones to take back with her.

"I've had breaks," he replied. "Not many, mind you, but I know when I need to step back so I don't get burnt out."

Catalina turned her face toward the ocean. She'd been burnt out on cleaning since she started. But sewing and designing, she could never imagine falling out of love with her passion.

They walked along in silence and Catalina let her thoughts run wild. What would've happened between them had Will not succumbed to his father's demands that he drop her? Would they have these romantic moments often? Would he make her take breaks from life and put work on hold for her?

She really couldn't see any of that, to be honest. Will was still under his father's thumb, whether he admitted it or not. He'd been at the house most mornings going over Rowling Energy stuff, which Catalina assumed was really just Will checking in.

"Why did you give up on us before?" she asked before she could think better of it.

Will stopped, causing Catalina to stop as well. She dropped his hand and turned to fully face him.

"Never mind," she said, shaking her head. "It doesn't matter now."

The muscle in Will's jaw ticked as he stared back at her. "It does matter. Our breakup damaged both of us."

Catalina pushed her hair behind her ears, which was useless as the wind kept whipping it out. "I'm pretty sure you weren't damaged, seeing as how ending our relationship was your decision."

When she started to walk on, Will gripped her elbow. "You think seeing you move on and dating another man wasn't crushing to me? You think knowing you were in another man's arms, maybe even in his bed, didn't tear me up?"

She'd tried not to think about Will when she threw herself into another relationship to mask the hurt. From the angst in his tone and the fire in his eyes, though... *had* Will been hurt over the breakup? How could that be when he was the one who had ultimately ended things? Did he not want the split? Was he doing it to appease his father? If that was the case then she was doubly angry that he hadn't fought for them.

"You thought I'd sit around and cry myself to sleep over you?" she retorted, refusing to feel guilt over a decision he'd made for both of them.

And so what if she'd shed tears over him? Many tears, in fact, but there was no way she'd admit such a thing. As far as he knew she was made of steel and stronger than her emotions.

"Besides, you had moved on quite nicely. You ended up in a relationship with a Montoro princess."

Dammit. She hadn't meant for that little green monster to slip out. Catalina knew just how much Bella and

James loved each other, yet there was that sliver of jealousy at the fact that Will had been all ready to put a ring on Bella's finger first.

Will laughed. "That fake engagement was a mistake from all angles. James and Bella have found something she never would've had with me."

"But you would've married her."

And that fact still bothered Catalina. She hated the jealousy she'd experienced when she'd discovered Will was engaged. Not that she ever thought she stood a chance, but how could anyone compete with someone as beautiful and sexy as Bella Montoro? She was not only royalty, she was a humanitarian with a good heart.

On a sigh, Catalina started walking again, concentrating on the shells lining the shore. "It doesn't matter, honestly. I shouldn't have brought it up."

She reached down to pick up an iridescent shell, smoothing her finger over the surface to swipe away the wet sand. Catalina slid the shell into the small hidden pocket on the side of her dress and kept walking, very much aware of Will at her side. He was a smart man not to deny her last statement. They both knew he would've married Bella because that's what his father had wanted. Joining the fortunes of the two dynamic families was Patrick's dream…the wrong son had fallen for the beauty, though.

They walked a good bit down the deserted beach. Catalina had no idea how Will had managed to find such a perfect place with total privacy, but he had no doubt planned this for a while. On occasion he would stop and find a shell for her, wordlessly handing it to her as they walked on. The tension was heavier now that she'd opened up the can of worms. She wished she'd kept her feelings to herself.

What did it matter if he was going to marry Bella? What man wouldn't want to spend his life with her? Not only that, had Catalina truly thought Will would remain single? Had she believed he was so exclusively focused on work that he wouldn't want to settle down and start the next generation of Rowling heirs?

The warm sun disappeared behind a dark cloud as the wind kicked into high gear. Catalina looked up and suppressed a groan. Of course a dark cloud would hover over her. The ominous sky was starting to match her mood.

"Should we head back to the yacht?" she asked, trying to tuck her wayward strands of hair behind her ears as she fought against the wind.

"I don't think it's going to do anything major. The forecast didn't show rain."

That nasty cloud seemed to indicate otherwise, but she wasn't going to argue. They already had enough on their plate.

Catalina glanced through the foliage, squinting as something caught her eye. "What's that?"

Will stopped and looked in the direction she'd indicated. "Looks like a cabin of sorts. I've not come this far inland before. Let's check it out."

Without waiting for her, Will took off toward the small building. Catalina followed, stepping over a piece of driftwood and trailing through the lush plants that had nearly overtaken the property.

"I wonder who had this cabin built," he muttered as he examined the old wood shack. "The island belongs to Alma from what I could tell when I first started coming here."

The covered porch leaned to one side, the old tin roof had certainly seen better days and some of the wood around the door and single window had warped. But the place had charm and someone had once cared enough to put it here. A private getaway for a couple in love? A hideout for someone seeking refuge from life? There was a story behind this place.

Will pushed on the door and eased inside. Catalina couldn't resist following him. The musty smell wasn't as bad as she'd expected, but the place was rather dusty. Only a bit of light from outside crept in through the single window, but even that wasn't bright because of the dark cloud covering.

"Careful," he cautioned when she stepped in. "Some of those boards feel loose."

There was enough dim light coming in the front window for them to see a few tarps, buckets and one old chair sitting against the wall.

"Looks like someone was working on this and it was forgotten," Catalina said as she walked around the room. "It's actually quite cozy."

Will laughed. "If you like the rustic, no-indoor-plumbing feel."

Crossing her arms over her chest, she turned around. "Some of us don't need to be pampered with amenities. I personally enjoy the basics."

"This is basic," he muttered, glancing around.

The sudden sound of rain splattering on the tin roof had Catalina freezing in place. "So much for that forecast."

Will offered her a wide smile. "Looks like you get to enjoy the basics a bit longer unless you want to run back to the yacht in the rain."

Crossing the room, Catalina sank down onto the old, sheet-covered chair. "I'm good right here. Will you be able to handle it?"

His aqua eyes raked over her, heating her skin just as effectively as if he'd touched her with his bare hands. "Oh, baby, I can handle it."

Maybe running back to the yacht was the better option after all. How long would she be stranded in an old shack with Will while waiting out this storm?

Catalina wasn't naïve. She knew full well there were only so many things they could talk about and nearly every topic between them circled back to the sexual tension that had seemed to envelop them and bind them together for the past several weeks.

Her body trembled as she kept her gaze locked onto his.

There was only one way this day would end.

Ten

William stared out the window at the sheets of rain coming down. He didn't need to look, though; the pounding on the roof told him how intense this storm was.

So much for that flawless forecast.

Still, staying across the room from Cat was best for now. He didn't need another invisible push in her direction. He glanced over his shoulder toward the woman he ached for. She sat as casual as you please with her legs crossed, one foot bouncing to a silent beat as her flip-flop dangled off her toes. Those bare legs mocked him. The strings of her bikini top peeking out of her dress mocked him as well. Every damn thing about this entire situation mocked him.

What had he been thinking, inviting her for a day out? Why purposely resurrect all of those old, unresolved feelings? They'd gone four years without bringing up their past, but Will had reached his breaking

point. He needed to know if they had a chance at…
what? What exactly did he want from her?

He had no clue, but he did know the need for Cat had
never lessened. If anything, the emptiness had grown
without her in his life. He'd let her go once to save her,
but he should've fought for them, fought for what he
wanted and found another way to keep her safe. He'd
been a coward. As humiliating as that was to admit,
there was no sugarcoating the truth of the boy he used
to be.

"You might as well have a seat," she told him, meeting his gaze. "The way you're standing across the room
is only making the tension worse. You're making me
twitchy."

Will laughed. Leave it to Cat to call him on his actions, though he didn't think the tension could get worse.

He crossed the room and took a seat on the floor in
front of the chair.

"This reminds me of that time James, you and I were
playing hide-and-seek when it started raining," she said.
"You guys were home from school on break and I had
come in to work with my mum."

Will smiled as the memory flooded his mind. "We
were around eight or nine, weren't we?"

Cat nodded. "James kept trying to hold my hand
when we both ran into the garage to hide and get dry."

Will sat up straighter. "You never told me that."

"Seriously?" she asked, quirking a brow. "You're
going to get grouchy over the actions of a nine-year-old?"

"I'm not grouchy. Surprised, but not grouchy."

"James was only doing it because he knew I had a
thing for you."

The corner of Will's mouth kicked up. "You had a
thing for me when you were that young?"

Cat shrugged, toying with the edge of her dress. "You were an older man. Practically worldly in all of your knowledge."

"It was the Spanish, wasn't it?" he asked with a grin.

Cat rolled her eyes and laughed. "James was fluent in Spanish as well. You two both had the same hoity-toity schooling."

Will lifted his knee and rested his arm on it as he returned her smile. "Nah. I was better. We would sometimes swap out in class because the teacher couldn't tell us apart. She just knew a quiet blond boy sat in the back. As long as one of us showed up, she didn't pay much attention to the fact there were really supposed to be two."

"Sneaky boys. But, I bet if I asked James about the Spanish speaking skills he'd say he was better," she countered.

"He'd be wrong."

Cat tipped her head, shifting in her seat, which only brought her bare legs within touching distance. "You tricked your teachers and got away with it. Makes me wonder how many times you two swapped out when it came to women."

Will shook his head. "I'm not answering that."

"Well, I know that watch nearly cost James the love of his life," Cat said, nodding toward the gold time-piece on his wrist.

"It was unfortunate Bella saw you and me kissing. I truly thought we were secluded." Will sighed and shifted on the wood floor. "She had every right to think James was kissing someone else because she had no clue about the bet."

The rain beat against the window as the wind kicked up. Cat tensed and her eyes widened.

"Hope this old place holds up," she said. "Maybe running back to the yacht would have been a better idea."

"Too late now." Will reached over, laying his hand on her knee. "We're fine. It's just a pop-up storm. You know these things pass fast."

With a subtle nod, she settled deeper into the seat and rested her head on the back cushion. Guilt rolled through Will. He'd planned a day for her, and had been hopeful that seduction would be the outcome. Yet here they sat in some abandoned old shack waiting out some freak storm. Even Mother Nature was mocking him.

But there was a reason they were here right now, during this storm, and Will wasn't going to turn this chance away. He planned on taking full advantage and letting Cat know just how much he wanted her.

Shifting closer to her chair, Will took Cat's foot and slid her shoe off. He picked up her other foot and did the same, all while knowing she had those dark, intoxicating eyes focused on his actions. It was her exotic eyes that hypnotized him.

Taking one of her delicate feet between his hands, Will started to massage, stroking his thumb up her arch.

"I'll give you ten minutes to stop that," she told him with a smile.

The radiant smile on her face was something he hadn't realized he'd missed so much. Right now, all relaxed and calm, even with the storm raging outside, Cat looked like the girl he once knew…the girl he'd wanted something more with.

But they were different people now. They had different goals. Well, he did; her goals were still unclear to him. He suddenly found himself wanting to know about those dreams of hers, and the fact that she'd hinted to James that she wouldn't stay in Alma forever.

But all of those questions could come later. Right now, Cat's comfort and happiness were all that mattered. Tomorrow's worries, issues and questions could be dealt with later. He planned on enjoying Cat for as long as she would allow.

Damn. When had this petite woman taken control over him? When had he allowed it? There wasn't one moment he could pinpoint, but there were several tiny instances where he could see in hindsight the stealthy buildup of her power over him.

Cat laughed as she slid down a bit further in the chair and gazed down at him beneath heavy lids. "If your father could see you on the floor rubbing his maid's feet, you'd lose your prestigious position at Rowling Energy."

Will froze, holding her gaze. It may have been a lighthearted joke, but there was so much truth to her statement about how angry this would make his father. But Will had already set in motion his plan to freeze his father out of the company.

Besides, right now, Will didn't care about Patrick or Rowling Energy. What he did care about was the woman who was literally turning to putty in his hands. Finally, he was going to show her exactly what they could be together and anticipation had his heart beating faster than ever.

"Does this feel good?" he asked.

Her reply was a throaty moan, sexy enough to have his body responding.

"Then all of the other stuff outside of this cabin doesn't matter."

Blinking down at him, Cat replied, "Not to me, but I bet if your father made you choose, you'd be singing a different tune."

Just like last time.

The unspoken words were so deafening, they actually drowned out the beating of the rain and the wind against the small shelter.

Will's best option was to keep any answer to himself. He could deny the fact, but he'd be lying. He'd worked too hard to get where he was to just throw it all away because of hormones.

At the same time, he planned on working equally as hard to win over Cat. There was no reason he had to give up anything.

His hand glided up to her ankle, then her calf. She said nothing as her eyes continued to hold his. He purposely watched her face, waiting for a sign of retreat, but all that was staring back at him was desire.

There was a silent message bouncing between them, that things were about to get very intimate, very fast.

The old cabin creaked and groaned against the wind's force. Cat tensed beneath him.

"You're safe," he assured her softly, not wanting to break this moment of trust she'd settled into with him. "This place is so old. I know it has withstood hurricanes. This little storm won't harm the cabin or us."

And there weren't any huge trees around, just thick bushes and flowers, so they weren't at risk for anything falling on them.

Right now, the only thing he needed to be doing was pushing through that line of defense Cat had built up. And from her sultry grin and heavy lids, he'd say he was doing a damn fine job.

Catalina should tell him to stop. Well, the common sense side of her told her she should. But the female side, the side that hadn't been touched or treasured in more time than she cared to admit, told her common sense to shut up.

Will had quite the touch. She had no idea the nerves in your feet could be so tied into all the girly parts. She certainly knew it now. Every part of her was zipping with ache and need. If he commanded her to strip and dance around the room naked, she would. The power he held over her was all-consuming and she was dying to know when he was going to do more.

She'd walked straight into this with her eyes wide open. So if she was having doubts or regrets already, she had no one to blame but herself. Though Catalina wasn't doubting or regretting. She was aching, on the verge of begging him to take this to the next level.

Catalina's head fell back against the chair as his hands moved to her other calf, quickly traveling up to her knee, then her thigh. She wanted to inch down further and part her legs just a tad, but that would be a silent invitation she wasn't quite brave enough for.

Yet.

"I've wanted to touch you for so long," he muttered, barely loud enough for her to hear over the storm. "I've watched you for the past four years, wondering if you ever thought of me. Wondering if you ever fantasized about me the way I did you."

Every. Single. Night.

Which was a confession she wasn't ready to share. The ball was in his court for now and she planned on just waiting to see how this played out.

He massaged her muscles with the tips of his fingers and the room became hotter with each stroke. If the man could have such power over her with something so simple as a foot massage, how would her body react once Will really started showing her affection?

"Do you remember that time your mother caught us making out?" he asked with a half laugh.

At the time, Catalina had been mortified that her mother caught them. But it wasn't until after the breakup that she realized why her mother had been so disappointed.

Patrick Rowling had really done a number on Catalina's mum. And it was those thoughts that could quickly put a bucket of cold water on this encounter, but she refused to allow Patrick to steal one more moment of happiness from her life...he'd already taken enough from her.

Will may not be down on his knees proposing marriage, but he was down on his knees showing her affection. And maybe she hoped that would be a stepping-stone to something more... But right now, that was all she wanted. She'd fought this pull toward him for too long. She hadn't wanted to let herself believe they could be more, but now she couldn't deny herself. She couldn't avoid the inevitable...she was falling for Will all over again.

"She didn't even know we were dating," Catalina murmured, her euphoric state suddenly overtaking her ability to speak coherently.

"Not many people did. That's when I realized I didn't want to keep us a secret anymore."

And that had been the start of their spiral toward the heartbreak she'd barely recovered from.

Once they were an "official" item, Patrick had intervened and put a stop to his good son turning to the maid. Shocking, since turning to the staff for pleasure certainly hadn't been below Patrick at one time. Not that what Catalina and Will shared had been anything like that. But the idea that Patrick could act as if he were so far above people was absolutely absurd.

"Don't tense on me now," Will warned. "You're supposed to be relaxing."

Catalina blew out a breath. "I'm trying. It's just hard when I'm stuck between the past and whatever is happening to us now."

Will came up to his knees, easing his way between her parted legs, his hands resting on the tops of her thighs, his fingertips brushing just beneath the hem of her dress.

"It's two different times. We're two different people. There's nothing to compare. Focus on now."

She stared down at those bright blue eyes, the wide open shirt and something dark against his chest. Was that...

"Do you have a tattoo?" she asked, reaching to pull back the shirt.

He said nothing as she eased the material aside. The glimpse she got wasn't enough. Catalina didn't ask, she merely gripped the shirt and pushed it off his shoulders. Will shifted until it fell to the floor.

Sure enough, black ink swirled over the left side of his chest and over his shoulder. She had no idea what the design was. All she knew was that it was sexy.

Without asking, she reached out and traced a thin line over his heart, then on up. The line thickened as it curled around his shoulder. Taut muscles tensed beneath her featherlight touch.

Catalina brought her gaze up to Will's. The intensity of his stare made her breath catch in her throat and stilled her hand.

"Don't stop," he whispered through clenched teeth.

"Will…"

His hand came up to cover hers. "Touch me, Cat."

He'd just handed her the reins.

With just enough pressure, he flattened her hand between his palm and his shoulder. The warmth of his skin penetrated her own, the heat sliding through her entire body.

"I—I want to but—"

She shook her head, killing the rest of her fears before they could be released and never taken back.

"But what?" he muttered, pushing her hair behind her ear, letting his fingertips trail over her cheek, her jawline and down her neck until she trembled.

"I'm not sure I can go any farther than that," she confessed. "I don't want to tease you."

"I've fantasized about you touching me like this for years. You're not teasing, you're fulfilling a fantasy."

Catalina stared into those aqua eyes and knew without a doubt he was serious. The fact that he'd been dreaming of her for this long confused her further, brought on even more questions than answers.

"Don't go there," he warned as if he knew where her thoughts were headed. "Keep touching me, Cat. Whatever happens here is about you and me and right this moment. Don't let past memories rob us of this time together."

Catalina opened her mouth, but Will placed one finger over her lips. "I have no expectations. Close your eyes."

Even though her heart beat out of control from anticipation and a slither of fear of the unknown, she did as he commanded.

"Now touch me. Just feel me, feel this moment and nothing else."

His tone might have been soft, but everything about

his words demanded that she obey. Not that he had to do much convincing. With her eyes closed, she wasn't forced to look at the face of the man who'd broken her heart. She wanted this chance to touch him, to ignore all the reasons why this was such a bad idea. But she couldn't look into those eyes and pretend that this was normal, that they were just two regular people stranded in an old shack.

With her eyes closed she actually felt as if they were regular people. She could pretend this was just a man she ached for, not a man who was a billionaire with more power than she'd ever see.

With her eyes closed she could pretend he wanted her for who she was and not just because she was a challenge.

Catalina brought her other hand up and over his chest. If she was given the green light to explore, she sure as hell wanted both hands doing the job. Just as she smoothed her palms up and over his shoulders, over his thick biceps, she felt the knot on her wrap dress loosen at her side.

Her eyes flew open. "What are you doing?"

"Feeling the moment."

The dress parted, leaving her torso fully exposed. "You don't play fair."

The heat in his eyes was more powerful than any passion she'd ever seen. "I never will when it comes to something I want."

"You said—"

"I'd never force you," he interrupted, gliding his fingertips over the straps of her bikini that stretched from behind her neck to the slopes of her breasts. "But that doesn't mean I won't try to persuade you."

As the rain continued to beat against the side of the

shack, Catalina actually found herself happy that she was stuck here. Perhaps this was the push she needed to follow through with what she truly wanted. No, she wasn't looking for happily-ever-after, she'd never be that naïve again where Will was concerned. But she was older now, was going into this with both eyes wide open.

And within the next couple months, hopefully she'd be out of Alma and starting her new life. So why not take the plunge now with a man she'd always wanted? Because he was right. This was all about them, here and now. Everything else could wait outside that door.

For now, Catalina was taking what she'd wanted for years.

Eleven

Catalina came to her feet. From here on out she was taking charge of what she'd been deprived of and what she wanted…and she wanted Will. Whatever doubts she had about sleeping with him wouldn't be near as consuming as the regret she'd have if she moved away and ignored this opportunity.

The moment she stood before him, Will sank back down on the floor and stared up at her as her dress fell into a puddle around her feet. As she stepped away and kicked the garment aside, his eyes roamed over her, taking in the sight of the bikini and nothing else.

The image of him sitting at her feet was enough to give her a sense of control, a sense of dominance. The one time when it counted most, she didn't feel inferior.

Will could've immediately taken over, he could've stood before her and taken charge, but he'd given her the reins.

"That bikini does some sinful things to your body." He reached out, trailed his fingertips over the sensitive area behind her knee and on up to her thigh. "Your curves are stunning, Cat. Your body was made to be uncovered."

"How long have you wanted me, Will?" she asked, needing to know this much. "Did you want me when we were together before?"

"More than anything," he rasped out, still sliding his fingers up and down the backs of her legs. "But I knew you were a virgin and I respected you."

"What if I were a virgin now?" she asked, getting off track. "Would you still respect me?"

"I've always respected you." He came up to his knees, putting his face level with her stomach. He placed a kiss just above her bikini bottoms before glancing up at her. "And I don't want to discuss if there's been another man in your bed."

With a move she hadn't expected, he tossed her back into the chair and stood over her, his hands resting on either side of her head. "Because I'm the only man you're going to be thinking of right now."

"I've only been with one other, but you're the only man I've ever wanted in my bed," she admitted. "I need you to know that."

Maybe she was naïve for letting him in on that little piece of information she'd kept locked in her heart for so long, but right now, something more than desire was sparking between them. He was too possessive for this to just be something quick and easy.

They weren't just scratching an itch, but she had no clue what label to put on what was about to happen. Which was why she planned on not thinking and just feeling. This bond that was forming here was something she'd have to figure out later…much later.

"All I need to know is that you want this as much as I do," he told her. "That you're ready for anything that happens because I can't promise soft and gentle. I've wanted you too long."

A shiver of arousal speared through her. "I don't need gentle, Will. I just need you."

In an instant his lips crushed hers. She didn't know when things had shifted, but in the span of about two minutes, she'd gone from questioning sex with Will to nearly ripping his shorts off so she could have him.

Will's strong hands gripped her hips as he shifted the angle of his head for a deeper kiss. Cat arched her body, needing to feel as much of him as possible. There still didn't seem to be enough contact. She wanted more… she wanted it all. The need to have everything she'd deprived herself of was now an all-consuming ache.

"Keep moaning like that, sweetheart," he muttered against her lips. "You're all mine."

She hadn't even realized she'd moaned, which just proved how much control this man had over her actions.

Gripping his shoulders, she tried to pull him down further, but he eased back. With his eyes locked onto hers, he hooked his thumbs in the waistband of his board shorts and shoved them to the floor. Stepping out of them he reached down, took her hand and pulled her to her feet.

Keeping her eyes on his, she reached behind her neck and untied her top. It fell forward as she worked on the knot. Soon they'd flung the entire scrap of fabric across the room. Will's eyes widened and his nostrils flared.

Excitement and anticipation roiled through her as she shoved her bottoms down without a care. She had no clue who reached for whom first, but the next second she was in his arms, skin to skin from torso to knees and she'd never felt anything better in her entire life.

Will's arms wrapped around her waist, his hands splaying across her bare back. He spun her around and sank down into the chair, pulling her down with him. Instinctively her legs straddled his hips. Catalina fisted her fingers in his hair as his lips trailed down her throat.

"So sexy," he murmured against her heated skin. "So mine."

Yes. She was his for now…maybe she always had been.

When his mouth found her breast, his hands encircled her hips. She waited, aching with need.

"Will," she panted, not recognizing her own voice. "Protection."

With his hair mussed, his lids heavy, he looked up. "I don't have any with me. Dammit, they're on the yacht. I didn't expect to get caught out here like this." Cursing beneath his breath, he shook his head. "I'm clean. I swear I wouldn't lie about something like that. I haven't been with a woman in…too long, and I recently had a physical."

"I know I'm clean and I'm on birth control."

He gave her a look, silently asking what she wanted to do. Without another word she slowly sank down onto him, so that they were finally, fully joined after years of wanting, years of fantasizing.

Their sighs and groans filled the small room. Wind continued to beat against the window as rain pelted the tin roof. Everything about this scenario was perfect. Even if they were in a rundown shed, she didn't care. The ambiance was amazingly right. The storm that had swept through them over the years only matched Mother

Nature's fury outside the door. This was the moment they were supposed to be together, this was what they'd both waited for so long.

"Look at me," he demanded, his fingertips pressing into her hips.

Catalina hadn't realized she'd closed her eyes, but she opened them and found herself looking into Will's bright, expressive aqua eyes. He may be able to hold back his words, but those eyes told her so much. Like the fact that he cared for her. This was sex, but there was so much more going on…so much more they'd discuss later.

As her hips rocked back and forth against his, Will continued to watch her face. Catalina leaned down, resting her hands on his shoulders. The need inside her built so fast, she dropped her forehead against his.

"No," he stated. "Keep watching me. I want to see your face."

As she looked back into his eyes, her body responded to every touch, every kiss, every heated glance. Tremors raced through her at the same time his body stilled, the cords in his neck tightened and his fingertips dug even further into her hips.

His body stiffened against hers, his lips thinned as his own climax took control. Catalina couldn't look away. She wanted to see him come undone, knowing she caused this powerful man to fall at the mercy of her touch.

Once their bodies eased out of the euphoric state, Catalina leaned down, rested her head on his shoulder and tried to regain some sense of normal breathing. She didn't know what to say now, how to act. They'd taken this awkward, broken relationship and put another speed bump in it. Now all they had to do was figure out how to maneuver over this new hurdle since they'd moved to a whole new, unfamiliar level.

Will trailed his hand up and down Cat's back, which was smooth and damp with sweat. Damn, she was sexier than he'd ever, *ever* imagined. She'd taken him without a second thought and with such confidence. Yet she'd been so tight…had she not slept with anyone? How had that not happened? Surely she wasn't still a virgin.

Had Cat kept her sexuality penned up all this time? For completely selfish reasons, this thought pleased him.

As much as Will wanted to know, he didn't want to say a word, didn't want to break the silence with anything that would kill the mood. The storm raged on outside, the cabin creaked and continued to groan under the pressure, but Cat was in his arms, her heart beating against his chest, and nothing could pull him from this moment.

The fact that he was concentrating on her heartbeat was a bit disconcerting. He didn't want to be in tune with her heart, he couldn't get that caught up with her, no matter how strong this invisible force was that was tugging him to her. Having her in his arms, finally making love to her was enough.

So why did he feel as if there was more to be had?

Because when he'd originally been thinking of the here and now, he'd somehow started falling into the zone of wanting more than this moment. He wanted Cat much longer than this day, this week, even. Will wanted more and now he had to figure out just how the hell that would work.

"Tell me I wasn't a substitute for Bella."

Will jerked beneath her, forcing her to sit up and meet his gaze. "What?"

Cat shook her head, smoothing her short hair away from her face. "Nothing," she said, coming to her feet. "That was stupid of me to say. We had sex. I'm not expecting you to give me anything more."

As she rummaged around the small space searching for her bikini and dress, Will sat there dumbfounded. So much for not letting words break the beauty of the moment.

What was that about Bella? Seriously? Did Cat honestly think that Will had had a thing for his brother's fiancée?

"Look at me," he demanded, waiting until Cat spun around, gripping her clothing to her chest. "Bella is married to James. I have no claim to her."

"It's none of my business."

Will watched as she tied her top on and slid the bikini bottoms up her toned legs. "It is your business after what we just did. I don't sleep with one woman and think of another."

Cat's dark eyes came up to his. A lock of her inky black hair fell over her forehead and slashed across her cheek.

"You owe me no explanations, Will." Hands on her hips, she blew the rogue strand from her face. "I know this wasn't a declaration of anything to come. I'm grown up now and I have no delusions that things will be any different than what they are. We slept together, it's over."

Okay, that had originally been his mindset when he'd gone into this, but when the cold words came from her mouth, Will suddenly didn't like the sound of it. She wasn't seeing how he'd changed at all and that was his fault. She still believed he was a jerk who had no cares at all for her feelings. But he did care...too damn much.

"I know you saw me as a challenge," she went on as she yanked the ties together to secure her dress. "A conquest, if you will. It's fine, really. I could've stopped you, but I was selfish and wanted you. So, thanks for—"

"Do not say another word." Pushing to his feet, Will jerked his shorts from the floor and tugged them on before crossing to her. "You can't lie to me, Cat. I know you too well. Whatever defense mechanism you're using here with ugly words isn't you. You're afraid of what you just felt, of what just happened. This wasn't just sex and you damn well know it."

Her eyes widened, her lips parted, but she immediately shut down any emotion he'd just seen flash across her face. No doubt about it, she was trying to cut him off before he did anything to hurt her...again. He should have seen this coming.

Guilt slammed into him. Not over sleeping with her just now, but for how she felt she had to handle the situation to avoid any more heartache.

"Will, I'm the maid," she said softly. "While I'm not ashamed of my position, I also know that this was just a onetime thing. A man like you would never think twice about a woman like me for anything more than sex."

Will gripped her arms, giving her a slight shake. "Why are you putting yourself into this demeaning little package and delivering it to me? I've told you more than once I don't care if you're a maid or a damn CEO. What just happened has nothing to do with anything other than us and what we feel."

"There is no us," she corrected him.

"There sure as hell was just a minute ago."

Why was he so dead set on correcting her? Here he

stood arguing with her when she was saying the same exact thing he'd been thinking earlier.

"And I have no clue why you're bringing Bella into this," he added.

Cat lifted her chin in a defiant gesture. "I'm a woman. Sometimes my insecurities come out."

"Why are you insecure about her?"

Cat laughed and broke free from his hold, taking a step back. "You were with one of the most beautiful women I've ever seen. Suddenly when that relationship is severed, you turn to me. You haven't given me any attention in nearly four years, Will. Forgive me if suddenly I feel like leftovers."

"Don't downgrade what just happened between us," he demanded. "Just because I didn't seek you out in the past few years doesn't mean I didn't want you. I wanted the hell out of you. And I was fighting my way back to you, dammit."

He eased closer, watching as her eyes widened when he closed the gap and loomed over her. "Seeing you all the time, being within touching distance but knowing I had no right was hell."

"You put yourself there."

As if he needed the reminder of the fool he'd been.

Will smoothed her hair back from her forehead, allowing his hand to linger on her jawline. "I can admit when I was wrong, stubborn and a jerk. I can also admit that I have no clue what just happened between us because it was much more than just sex. You felt it, I felt it, and if we deny that fact we'd just be lying to ourselves. Let's get past that. Honesty is all we can have here. We deserve more than something cheap, Cat."

Cat closed her eyes and sighed. When her lids lifted,

she glanced toward the window. "The rain has let up. We should head back to the yacht."

Without another word, without caring that he was standing here more vulnerable than he'd ever been, Cat turned, opened the door and walked out.

Nobody walked out on Will Rowling and he sure as hell wasn't going to let the woman he was so wrapped up in and had just made love to be the first.

Twelve

Catalina had known going into this day that they'd most likely end up naked and finally giving into desires from years ago.

And she hadn't been able to stop herself.

No matter what she felt now, no matter what insecurities crept up, she didn't regret sleeping with Will.

This was a one and done thing—it had to be. She couldn't afford to fall any harder for this man whom she couldn't have. She was planning on leaving Alma anyway, so best to cut ties now and start gearing up for her fresh start. Letting her heart interfere with the dreams she'd had for so long would only have her working backward. She was so close, she'd mentally geared up for the break from Alma, from Will…but that was before she'd given herself to him.

But what had just transpired between them was only closure. Yes, that was the term she'd been looking for.

Closure. Nothing else could come from their intimacy and finally getting each other out of their systems was the right thing to do...wasn't it?

While the rain hadn't fully stopped, Catalina welcomed the refreshing mist hitting her face. She had no clue of the amount of time that had passed while they'd been inside the cabin lost in each other. An hour? Three hours?

The sand shifted beneath her bare feet as she marched down the shore toward the dock. Sandals in her hand, she kept her focus on the yacht in the distance and not the sound of Will running behind her. She should've known he'd come chasing after her, and not just because he wanted to get back to the yacht.

She'd left no room for argument when she'd walked out, and Will Rowling wouldn't put up with that. Too bad. She was done talking. It was time to move on.

Too bad her body was still humming a happy tune and tingling in all the areas he'd touched, tasted.

Figuring he'd grab her when he caught up to her, Catalina turned, ready to face down whatever he threw her way. Will took a few more steps, stopping just in front of her. He was clutching his wadded up shirt at his side. Catalina couldn't help but stare at his bare chest and the mesmerizing tattoo as he pulled in deep breaths.

"You think we're done?" he asked as he stared her down. "Like we're just heading back to the yacht, setting off to Alma and that's it? You think this topic is actually closed? That I would accept this?"

Shrugging, Catalina forced herself to meet his angry gaze. "You brought me here to seduce me. Wasn't that the whole plan for getting me alone? Well, mission accomplished. The storm has passed and it'll start getting dark in a couple hours. Why wait to head back?"

"Maybe because I want to spend more time with you," he shouted. "Maybe because I want more here than something cheap and easy."

As the misty rain continued to hit her face, Catalina wanted to let that sliver of hope into her heart, but she couldn't allow it…not just yet. "And what do you want, Will? An encore performance? Maybe in your bed on the yacht so you can have a more pampered experience?"

His lips thinned, the muscle in his jaw tightened. "What made you so harsh, Cat? You weren't like this before."

Before when she'd been naïve, before when she'd actually thought he may love her and choose her over his career. And before she discovered a secret that he still knew nothing about.

Beyond all of that, she was angry with herself for allowing her emotions to get so caught up in this moment. She should've known better. She'd never been someone to sleep around, but she thought for sure she could let herself go with Will and then walk away. She'd been wrong and now because of her roller coaster of emotions, she was taking her anger out on him.

Shaking her head, Catalina turned. Before she could take a step, she tripped over a piece of driftwood she hadn't seen earlier. Landing hard in the sand, she hated how the instant humiliation took over.

Before she could become too mortified, a spearing pain shot through her ankle. She gasped just as Will crouched down by her side.

"Where are you hurt?" he asked, his eyes raking over her body.

"My ankle," she muttered, sitting up so she could look at her injury.

"Anywhere else?" Will asked.

Catalina shook her head as she tried to wiggle her ankle back and forth. Bad idea. She was positive it wasn't broken—she'd broken her arm as a little girl and that pain had been much worse—but she was also sure she wouldn't be able to apply any pressure on it and walk. The piercing pain shot up her leg and had her wincing. She hoped she didn't burst into tears and look even more pathetic.

So much for her storming off in her dramatic fit of anger.

Will laid his shirt on her stomach.

"What—?"

Before she could finish her question, he'd scooped her up in his arms and set off across the sand. Catalina hated how she instantly melted against his warm, bare chest. Hated how the image of them in her mind seemed way more romantic than what it was, with Will's muscles straining as he carried her in his arms—yeah, they no doubt looked like something straight out of a movie.

"You can't carry me all the way to the yacht," she argued. "This sand is hard enough to walk in without my added weight."

"Your weight is perfect." He threw her a glance, silently leaving her no room for argument. "Relax and we'll see what we're dealing with once I can get you on the bed in the cabin."

Those words sent a shiver of arousal through her that she seriously did not want. Hadn't she learned from the last set of shivers? Hadn't she told herself that after they slept together she'd cut ties? She had no other choice, not if she wanted to maintain any dignity and sanity on her way out of his life for good.

As they neared the dock, Will was breathing hard,

but he didn't say a word as he trudged forward. Her ankle throbbed, which should have helped shift her focus, but being wrapped in Will's strong arms pretty much overrode any other emotion.

Catalina had a sinking feeling that in all her pep talks to herself, she'd overlooked the silent power Will had over her. She may have wanted to have this sexcapade with him and then move on, but she'd seriously underestimated how involved her heart would become.

And this hero routine he was pulling was flat-out sexy…as if she needed another reason to pull her toward him.

Will quickly crossed toward the dock, picking up his pace now that he was on even ground. When he muttered a curse, Catalina lifted her head to see what the problem was. Quickly she noted the damage to the yacht and the dock. Apparently the two had not played nice during the freak storm.

"Oh, Will," she whispered.

He slowed his pace as he carefully tested the weight of the dock. Once his footing was secure, and it was clear that the planks would hold them, he cautiously stepped forward.

"I need to set you down for a second to climb on board, but just keep pressure off that ankle and hold onto my shoulders."

She did as he asked and tried not to consider just what this damage meant for their return trip home. When Will was on deck, he reached out, proceeded to scoop her up again and lifted her onto the yacht.

"I can get down the steps," she told him, really having no clue if she could or not. But there was no way they could both fit through that narrow doorway to get below deck. "Go figure out what happened."

He kept his hold firm. "I'm going to get you settled, assess your ankle and then go see what damage was done to the yacht."

Somehow he managed to get her down the steps and onto the bed without bumping her sore, now swollen ankle along the way. As he adjusted the pillows behind her, she slid back to lean against the fluffy backdrop. Will took a spare pillow and carefully lifted her leg to elevate her injury.

"It's pretty swollen," he muttered as he stalked toward the galley kitchen and returned with a baggie full of ice wrapped in a towel. "Keep this on it and I'll go see if I can find some pain reliever."

"Really, it'll be fine," she lied. The pain was bad, but she wanted him to check on the damage so they could get back to Alma… She prayed they could safely get back. "Go see how bad the destruction is. I'm not going anywhere."

Will's brows drew in. With his hands on his hips, that sexy black ink scrolling over his bare chest and the taut muscles, he personified sex appeal.

"Staring at my ankle won't make it any better," she told him, suddenly feeling uncomfortable.

His unique blue eyes shifted and held her gaze. "I hate that I hurt you," he muttered.

So much could be read from such a simple statement. Was he referring to four years ago? Did he mean the sexual encounter they'd just had or was he referencing her fall?

No matter what he was talking about, Catalina didn't want to get into another discussion that would only take them in circles again. They were truly getting nowhere…well, they'd ended up naked, but other than that, they'd gotten nowhere.

"Go on," she insisted. "Don't worry about me."

He looked as if he wanted to argue, but ended up nodding. "I'll be right back. If you need something, just yell for me. I'll hear you."

Catalina watched as he ascended the steps back up to the deck. Closing her eyes, she dropped her head against the pillows and pulled in a deep breath. If the storm had done too much damage to the yacht, she was stuck. Stuck on a glamorous yacht with an injured ankle with the last person she should be locked down with.

The groan escaped before she could stop it. Then laughter followed. Uncontrollable laughter, because could they be anymore clichéd? The maid and the millionaire, stranded on a desert island. Yeah, they had the makings for a really ridiculous story or some skewed reality show.

Once upon a time she would've loved to have been stranded with Will. To know that nothing would interrupt them. They could be who they wanted to be without pretenses. Just Will and Catalina, two people who I—

No. They didn't love each other. That was absurd to even think. Years ago she had thought they were in love, but they couldn't have been. If they'd truly been in love, wouldn't he have fought for everything they'd discussed and dreamed of?

Maybe he'd been playing her the entire time. A twenty-year-old boy moving up the ladder of success really didn't have much use for a poor staff member. She was a virgin and an easy target. Maybe that's all he'd been after.

But she really didn't think so. She'd grown up around Will and James. James was the player, not Will. Will had always been more on the straight and narrow, the rule follower.

And he'd followed those rules right to the point of breaking her heart. She should have seen it coming, really. After their mother passed away, Will did every single thing he could to please his father, as if overcompensating for the loss of a parent.

Yet there was that little girl fantasy in her that had held out hope that Will would see her as more, that he would fall in love with her and they could live happily ever after.

Catalina sighed. That was long ago; they were different people now and the past couldn't be redone...and all those other stupid sayings that really didn't help in the grand scheme of things.

And it was because she was still so tied up in knots over this man that she needed to escape Alma, fulfill her own dreams and forget her life here. She was damn good at designing and she couldn't wait to burn her uniforms and sensible shoes, roast a marshmallow over them and move on.

"We're not going anywhere for a while."

Catalina jerked her head around. Will was standing on the bottom step, his hands braced above him on the doorframe. The muscles in his biceps flexed, drawing her attention to his raw masculinity. No matter how much the inner turmoil was caused by their rocky relationship, Catalina couldn't deny that the sight of his body turned her on like no other man had ever been able to do.

"There's some major damage to the starboard side. I thought maybe I could get it moving, but the mechanics are fried. I can only assume the boat was hit by lightning as well as banging into the dock repeatedly."

Catalina gripped the plush comforter beneath her palms. "How long will we be stuck here?"

"I have no clue."

He stepped farther into the room and raked a hand over his messy hair. Will always had perfectly placed hair, but something about that rumpled state made her hotter for him.

"The radio isn't working, either," he added as he sank down on the edge of the bed, facing her. "Are you ready for some pain medicine since we're going to be here awhile?"

She was going to need something a lot stronger if she was going to be forced to stick this out with him for too long. Hours? Days? How long would she have to keep her willpower on high alert?

"I probably better," she admitted. "My ankle's throbbing pretty good now."

Will went to the bathroom. She heard him rummaging around in a cabinet, then the faucet. When he strode back across the open room, Catalina couldn't keep her eyes off his bare chest. Why did he have to be so beautiful and enticing? She wanted to be over her attraction for this man. Anything beyond what happened in that cabin would only lead to more heartache because Will would never choose anyone over his father and Rowling Energy and she sure as hell wasn't staying in Alma to clean toilets the rest of her life waiting to gain his attention.

Catalina took the pills and the small paper cup of water he offered. Hoping the medicine kicked in soon, she swallowed it as Will eased back down beside her on the bed.

"Dammit," he muttered, placing his hand on the shin of her good leg. "If we hadn't been arguing—"

"We've argued for weeks," she told him with a half smile. "It was an accident. If anyone is to blame it's me for not watching where I was going and for trying to stomp off in a fit."

"Were you throwing a fit?" he asked. "I don't remember."

Catalina lifted an eyebrow. "You're mocking me now."

Shaking his head, he slid his hand up and down her shin. "Not at all. I just remember thinking how sexy you looked when you were angry. You have this red tint to your cheeks. Or it could've been the great sex. Either way, you looked hot."

"Was that before or after I was sprawled face first in the sand?" she joked, trying to lighten the mood.

"You can't kill sexy, Cat, even if you're eating sand."

The slight grin he offered her eased her worry. Maybe they could spend the day here and actually be civil without worrying about the sexual tension consuming them. Maybe they had taken the edge off and could move on.

Well, they could obviously move on, but would this feeling of want ever go away? Because if anything, since they'd been intimate, Catalina craved him even more.

So now what could she do? There was nowhere to hide and definitely nowhere to run in her current state.

As she looked into Will's mesmerizing eyes, her worry spiked once again because he stared back at her like a man starved…and she was the main course.

Thirteen

Thankfully the kitchen was fully stocked and the electricity that fed the appliances hadn't been fried because right now Will needed to concentrate on something other than how perfect Cat looked in his bed.

He'd come to the kitchen a while ago to figure out what they should do for dinner. Apparently the pain pills had kicked in because Cat was resting peacefully, even letting out soft moans every now and then as she slept.

It was those damn moans that had his shorts growing tighter and his teeth grinding as he attempted to control himself. He'd heard those groans earlier, up close and personal in his ear as she'd wrapped her body around his.

The experience was one he would never forget.

Will put together the chicken and rice casserole that his mother used to make. Yes, they'd had a chef when he was a child, but James and Will had always loved this dish and every now and then, Will threw it together just to remember his mother. He still missed her, but it was the little things that would remind him of her and make him smile.

Setting the timer on the oven, Will glanced back to the sleeping beauty in his bed. His mother would have loved Cat. She wouldn't have cared if she was the maid or—

What the hell? How did that thought sneak right in without his realizing the path his mind was taking? It didn't matter what his mother would have thought of Cat. He wasn't getting down on one knee and asking her into the family.

He needed to get a grip because his hormones and his mind were jumbling up all together and he was damn confused. Sleeping with Cat should have satisfied this urge to claim her, but instead of passing, the longing only grew.

With the casserole baking for a good bit, Will opted to grab a shower. He smelled like sex, sand and sweat. Maybe a cold shower would help wake him up to the reality that he'd let Cat go once. Just because they slept together didn't mean she was ready to give this a go again. And was that what he wanted? In all honesty did he want to try for this once more and risk hurting her, hurting himself, further?

He was making a damn casserole for pity's sake. What type of man had he become? He'd turned into some warped version of a homemaker and, even worse, he was perfectly okay with this feeling.

Before he went to the shower, he wanted to try the radio one more time. There had to be a way to communicate back to the mainland. Unfortunately, no matter which knobs he turned, which buttons he hit, nothing sparked to life. Resigned to the fact they were indeed stuck, Will went to his master suite bathroom.

As he stripped from his shorts and stepped into the spacious, open shower, he wondered if maybe being stranded with Cat wasn't some type of sign. Maybe they were supposed to be together with no outside forces hindering their feelings or judgment.

And honestly, Will wanted to see what happened with Cat. He wanted to give this another chance because they were completely different people than they were before and he was in total control of his life. She was that sliver of happiness that kept him smiling and their verbal sparring never failed to get him worked up.

No other woman matched him the way she did and he was going to take this opportunity of being stranded and use every minute to his advantage. He'd prove to her he was different because just telling her he was really wouldn't convince her. He needed to show her, to let her see for herself that he valued her, that he wanted her. He'd never stopped wanting her.

While he may want to use this private time to seduce the hell out of her, Will knew those hormones were going to have to take a back seat because Cat was worth more and they were long overdue for some relaxing, laid back time. And then maybe they could discuss just what the hell was happening between them.

Whatever that smell was, Catalina really hoped she wasn't just dreaming about it. As soon as she opened her eyes, she was greeted with a beautiful orange glow across the horizon. The sun was setting, and lying in this bed, Will's bed, watching such beauty was a moment she wanted to lock in her mind forever.

She rolled over, wincing as the pain in her ankle reminded her she was injured. The ice bag had melted and slid off the pillow she'd propped it on. As soon as she sat up, she examined her injury, pleased to see the swelling had gone down some.

"Oh, good. Dinner is almost ready."

Catalina smoothed her hair away from her face and smiled as Will scooped up something from a glass pan.

"I tried the radio again," he told her. "It didn't work. The whole system is fried."

Catalina sighed. As much as she wanted to get back home, she couldn't deny the pleasure she'd experienced here, despite the injury. She had a feeling she was seeing the true Will, the man who wasn't all business and power trips, but a man who cared for her whether he was ready to admit it or not.

"Someone will come for us," she told him. "Besides, with you cooking and letting me nap, you're spoiling me. Dinner smells a lot like that chicken dish you made me for our first date."

Will grinned back at her and winked. *Winked.* What had she woken to? Will in the kitchen cooking and actually relaxed enough to wink and smile as if he hadn't a care in the world.

"It is," he confirmed. "I'll bring it to you so don't worry about getting up."

"I actually need to go to the restroom."

In seconds, Will was at her side helping her up. When he went to lift her in his arms, she pushed against him.

"Just let me lean on you, okay? No need to carry me."

Wrapping an arm around her waist, Will helped her stand. "How's the ankle feeling?"

"Really sore, but better than it was." She tested it, pulling back when the sharp throbbing started again.

"Putting weight on it still isn't a smart move, but hopefully it will be much better by tomorrow."

Will assisted her across the room, but when they reached the bathroom doorway, she placed a hand on his chest. "I can take it from here."

No way was he assisting her in the bathroom. She'd like to hold onto some shred of dignity. Besides, she needed a few moments to herself to regain mental footing since she was stuck playing house with the only man she'd ever envisioned spending forever with.

"I'll wait right here in case you need something," he told her. "Don't lock the door."

With a mock salute, Catalina hobbled into the bathroom and closed the door. The scent of some kind of masculine soap assaulted her senses. A damp towel hung over the bar near the shower. He'd made use of the time she'd been asleep. Her eyes darted to the bathtub that looked as if it could seat about four people. What she wouldn't give to crawl into that and relax in some hot water, with maybe a good book or a glass of wine. When was the last time she'd indulged in such utterly selfish desires?

Oh, yeah, when she'd stripped Will naked and had her way with him in the old cabin earlier today.

A tap on the door jerked her from her thoughts. "Are you okay?"

"Yeah. Give me a minute."

A girl couldn't even fantasize in peace around here. She still needed time to process what their intimacy meant and the new, unexpected path their relationship had taken. Will had most likely thought of what happened the entire time she'd been asleep. Of course he was a man, so he probably wasn't giving their encounter the amount of mind space she would.

Minutes later, Catalina opened the door to find Will leaning against the frame. Once again he wrapped an arm around her and steered her toward the bed.

"I can eat at the table." She hated leaning on him, touching him when her nerves were still a jumbled up mess. "I'm already up. That bed is too beautiful to eat on."

In no time he'd placed their plates on the table with two glasses of wine...again, her favorite. A red Riesling.

"If I didn't know better, I'd say you stocked this kitchen just for me," she joked as she took her first sip and knew it wasn't the cheap stuff she kept stocked in her fridge.

"I did buy a lot of things I knew you liked." His fork froze midway to his mouth as he looked up at her. "At least, you liked this stuff four years ago."

For a split second, he seemed unsure. Will was always confident in everything, but when discussing her tastes, he suddenly doubted himself. Why did she find that so adorable?

She felt a shiver travel up her spine. She didn't have time for these adorable moments and couldn't allow them to influence her where this man was concerned. That clean break she wanted couldn't happen if she let herself be charmed like that.

They ate in silence, but Catalina was surprised the strain wasn't there. Everything seemed...normal. Something was up. He wasn't trying to seduce her, he wasn't bringing up the past or any other hot topic.

What had happened while she'd been asleep? Will had suddenly transformed into some sort of caretaker with husbandlike qualities.

But after a while she couldn't take the silence anymore. Catalina dropped her fork to her empty plate.

"That was amazing. Now, tell me what's going through your mind."

Will drained his glass before setting it back down and focusing on her. "Right now I'm thinking I could use dessert."

"I mean why are you so quiet?"

Shrugging, he picked up their plates and put them in the kitchen. When he brought back the wine bottle, she put a hand over hers to stop him from filling her glass back up.

"If I need more pain pills later, it's best I don't have any more even though I only took a half pill."

Nodding, he set the bottle on the table and sat across from her again.

"Don't ignore the question."

A smile kicked up at the corners of his mouth. "I'm plotting."

Catalina eased back in her seat, crossing her arms over her chest. "You're always plotting. I take it I'm still in the crosshairs?"

His eyes narrowed in that sexy, toe-curling way that demanded a woman take notice. "You've never been anywhere else."

Her heart beat faster. When he said those things she wanted to believe him. She wanted to be the object of his every desire and fantasy. And when he looked at her as if nothing else in the world mattered, she wanted to stay in that line of sight forever, though she knew all of that was a very naïve way of thinking.

"I only set out to seduce you," he went on, toying with the stem on his glass. "I wanted you in my bed more than anything. And now that I've had you…"

Catalina wished she'd had that second glass of wine after all. "What are you saying?"

His intense stare locked onto her. "We're different people. Maybe we're at a stage where we can learn from the past and see…"

It took every ounce of her willpower not to lean forward in anticipation as his words trailed off yet again. "And see what?" she finally asked.

"Maybe I want to see where we could go."

Catalina gasped. "You're not serious."

Those heavy-lidded eyes locked onto her. "I can't let you go now that I know how right we are together."

Her eyes shifted away and focused on the posh living space while she tried to process all he was saying.

Her mother's words of warning from years ago echoed in Catalina's mind. How could she fall for this man with his smooth words and irresistible charm? Hadn't her mother done the same thing with Patrick?

No. Will wasn't Patrick and Catalina was not her mother.

To her knowledge, Will, even to this day, had absolutely no idea what had transpired when he'd been a young boy right around the time of his mother's death. That hollow pit in Catalina's stomach deepened. Had the affair been the catalyst in Mrs. Rowling's death?

"Why now?" she asked, turning back to face him. "Why should I let you in now after all this time? Is it because I'm convenient? Because I'm still single or because you're settling?"

Why was fate dangling this right in front of her face when she'd finally decided to move on? It had taken her years to get up the nerve to really move forward with her dream and now that she'd decided to take a chance, Will wanted back in?

"Trust me, you're anything but convenient," he laughed.

"I've busted my butt trying to think of ways to get your attention."

Catalina swallowed. "But why?"

"Because you want this just as much as I do," he whispered.

Catalina stared down at her hands clasped in her lap. "We're at the age now that our wants don't always matter." Letting her attention drift back up, she locked her eyes on him. "We both have different goals, Will. In the end, nothing has really changed."

"On that we can agree." Will came to his feet, crossed to her side of the table and loomed over her. His hands came to rest on the back of her chair on either side of her shoulders. "In the end, I'll still want you and you'll still want me. The rest can be figured out later."

Before she could say anything, he'd scooped her up in his arms. "Don't say a word," he chided. "I want to carry you, so just let me. Enjoy this moment, that's all I'm asking. Don't think about who we are away from here. Let me care for you the way you deserve."

His warm breath washed over her face as she stared back at him. He didn't move, he just waited for her reply.

What could she say? He was right. They both wanted each other, but was that all this boiled down to? There were so many other outside factors driving a wedge between them. Did she honestly believe that just because he said so things would be different?

Catalina stared into those eyes and for once she saw hope; she saw a need that had nothing to do with sex.

Resting her head on his shoulder, Catalina whispered, "One of us is going to get hurt."

Fourteen

Catalina leaned back against Will's chest as they set-tled onto the oversized plush sofa on the top deck. The full moon provided enough light and just the perfect ambiance; even Will couldn't have planned it better.

Granted he didn't like that the yacht was damaged or that Catalina had been injured, but the feel of her wrapped in his arms, their legs intertwined, even as he was careful of her ankle, was everything he'd wanted since he let her walk away so long ago.

Will laced his hands over her stomach and smiled when she laid her hands atop his.

"It's so quiet and peaceful," she murmured. "The stars are so vibrant here. I guess I never pay much at-tention in Alma."

"One of these days you're going to have your own maid, your own staff," he stated firmly. "You deserve to be pampered for all the hours you work without asking for anything in return. You work too hard."

"I do," she agreed. "I have so many things I want to do with my life and working is what keeps me motivated."

A strand of her hair danced in the breeze, tickling his cheek, but he didn't mind. Any way he could touch her and be closer was fine with him. She wasn't trying to ignore this pull and she'd actually relaxed fully against him. This is what they needed. The simplicity, the privacy.

"What are your goals, Cat?"

"I'd love a family someday."

The wistfulness in her tone had him wanting to fulfill those wishes. Will knew he'd never be able to sit back and watch her be with someone else, make a life and a family with another man.

"What else?" he urged. "I want to know all of your dreams."

She stiffened in his arms. Will stroked her fingers with his, wanting to keep her relaxed, keep her locked into this euphoric moment.

"It's just me, Cat." He purposely softened his tone. "Once upon a time we shared everything with each other."

"We did. I'm just more cautious now."

Because of him. He knew he'd damaged that innocence in her, he knew full well that she was a totally different woman because of his selfish actions. And that fact was something he'd have to live with for the rest of his life. All he could do was try to make things better now and move forward.

"I shouldn't have let you go," he muttered before he could think.

"Everything happens for a reason."

Will didn't miss the hint of pain in her tone. "Maybe so, but I should've fought for you, for us."

"Family has always been your top priority, Will. You've been that way since your mother passed. You threw yourself into pleasing your father and James ran wild. Everyone grieves differently and it's affected your relationships over the years."

Will shouldn't have been surprised that she'd analyzed him and his brother so well. Cat had always been so in tune with other people's feelings. Had he ever done that for her? Had he ever thought of her feelings if they didn't coincide with his own wants and needs?

"I never wanted you hurt." Yet he'd killed her spirit anyway. "I have no excuse for what I did. Nothing I say can reverse time or knock sense into the man I was four years ago."

"Everything that happened made me a better person." She shifted a bit and lifted her ankle to resettle it over the edge of the sofa. "I poured myself into new things, found out who I really am on my own. I never would've done that had I been with you."

Will squeezed her tighter. "I wouldn't have let you lose yourself, Cat. Had you been with me I would've pushed you to do whatever you wanted."

She tipped her head back and met his gaze. "You wouldn't have let me work. You would've wanted the perfect, doting wife."

There was a ring of truth to her words. He most likely would have tried to push her into doing what he thought was best.

"I wasn't good to you." He swallowed. "You were better off without me, but it killed me to let you go, knowing you'd be fine once you moved on."

Silence settled heavily around them before she finally said, "I wasn't fine."

"You were dating a man two months after we broke up."

Cat turned back around, facing the water. "I needed to date, I needed to move on in any way that I could and try to forget you. When I was alone my mind would wander and I'd start to remember how happy I was with you. I needed to fill that void in any way I possibly could."

Will swallowed. He'd hated seeing her with another man, hated knowing he was the one who drove her into another's arms.

"I slept with him."

Her words cut through the darkness and straight to his heart. "I don't want—"

"I slept with him because I was trying to forget you," she went on as if he hadn't said a word. "I was ready to give myself to you, then you chose to obey your father once again at my expense. When I started dating Bryce, I mistook his affection for love. I knew I was on the rebound, but I wanted so badly to be with someone who valued me, who wanted to be with me and put me first."

Those raw, heartfelt words crippled him. He'd had no idea just how much damage he'd caused. All this time, she'd been searching for anyone to put her at the top of their priority list when he'd shoved her to the bottom of his.

"Afterward I cried," she whispered. "I hated that I'd given away something so precious and I hated even more that I still wished I'd given it to you."

Her honesty gutted him. Will wished more than anything he could go back and make changes, wished he could go back and be the man she needed him to be.

But he could be honest now, he could open up. She'd shared such a deep, personal secret, he knew she deserved to know why he'd let her go so easily.

"I had to let you go."

"I know, your father—"

"No." Will adjusted himself in the seat so he could face her better. "I need you to know this, I need you to listen to what I'm saying. I let you go because of my father, but not for the reasons you think."

The moon cast enough of a glow for Will to see Cat's dark eyes widen. "What?"

"I let you go to save you. My father's threats…" Will shook his head, still angry over the way he'd let his father manipulate him. "As soon as I let you go, I was plotting to get you back, to put my father in his place. I didn't care how long it took, didn't care what I had to do."

Cat stared back at him, and he desperately wanted to know what was swirling around in her head. There was so much hurt between them, so many questions and years of resentment. Will hated his father for putting him in this position, but he hated even more the way Cat had been the victim in all of this.

"Your father threatened me, didn't he?" Cat asked, her voice low, yet firm. "He held me over your head? Is that why you let me go?"

Swallowing the lump of guilt, Will nodded.

Cat sat up, swung her feet over the side and braced her hands on either side of her hips. Will lifted his leg out of her way and brought his knee up to give her enough room to sit. He waited while she stared down at the deck. Silence and moonlight surrounded them, bathing them in a peace that he knew neither of them felt.

"Talk to me." He couldn't handle the uncertainty. "I don't want you going through this alone."

A soft laugh escaped her as she kept her gaze averted. "But you didn't care that I went through this alone four years ago."

"Dammit, Cat. I couldn't let you get hurt. He had the ability to ruin you and I wasn't going to put my needs ahead of yours."

When she threw him a glance over her shoulder, Will's gut tightened at the moisture gathered in her eyes. "You didn't put my needs first at all. You didn't give me a chance to fight for us and you took the easy way out."

Raking a hand over his hair, Will blew out a breath. "I didn't take the easy way," he retorted. "I took the hardest way straight through hell to keep you safe and to work on getting you back."

She continued to stare, saying nothing. Moments later her eyes widened. "Wait," she whispered. "How did Bella come into play?"

"You know I never would've married her. That was all a farce to begin with." Will shifted closer, reaching out to smooth her hair back behind her ear. "And once I kissed you, I knew exactly who I wanted, who I needed."

Cat started to stand, winced and sat back down. Will said nothing as he pushed his leg around her, once again straddling her from behind. He pulled her back against his chest and leaned on the plush cushions. Even though she remained rigid, he knew the only way to get her to soften was for him to be patient. He'd waited four years; he was the epitome of patient.

Wrapping his arms around her, he whispered in her ear. "I messed up," he admitted. "I only wanted to protect you and went about it the wrong way. Don't shut me out now, Cat. We have too much between us. This goes so much deeper than either of us realizes and I won't let my father continue to ruin what we have."

Dammit, somewhere along the way to a heated affair Will had developed stronger feelings, a deeper bond with Cat than he'd anticipated. And now that he knew he wanted more from her, he was close to losing it all.

"And what do we have, Will?" Her words came out on a choked sob.

"What do you want?"

What do you want?

Catalina couldn't hold in the tension another second. There was only so much one person could handle and Will's simple question absolutely deflated her. Melting back against his body once more, she swallowed the emotion burning her throat.

"I want…" Catalina shut her eyes, trying to figure out all the thoughts fighting for head space. "I don't know now. Yesterday I knew exactly what I wanted. I was ready to leave Alma to get it."

Will's fingertips slid up and down her bare arms, causing her body to tremble beneath his delicate touch. "And now? What do you want now, Cat?"

Everything.

"I don't want to make things harder for you," he went on. "But I'm not backing down. Not this time."

And there was a portion of her heart that didn't want him to. How could she be so torn? How could two dreams be pulling her in completely different directions?

Because the harder she'd tried to distance herself from him, the more she was being pulled back in.

"I'm afraid," she whispered. "I can't make promises and I'm not ready to accept them from you, either."

His hands stilled for the briefest of moments before he kissed the top of her head. Catalina turned her cheek to rest against his chest, relishing the warmth of his body, the strong steady heartbeat beneath her. Part of her wanted to hate him for his actions years ago, the other part of her wanted to cry for the injustice of it all.

But a good portion of her wanted to forgive him, to believe him when he said that he'd sacrificed himself to keep her safe. Why did he have to be so damn noble and why hadn't he told her to begin with? He didn't have to fight that battle all on his own. Maybe she could have saved him, too.

Catalina closed her eyes as the yacht rocked steadily to the soothing rhythm of the waves. She wanted to lock this moment in time and live here forever. Where there were no outside forces trying to throw obstacles in their way and the raw honesty...

No. She still carried a secret that he didn't know and how could she ever tell him? How could she ever reveal the fact that his father had had an affair with her mother? Would he hate her for knowing?

"Will, I need—"

"We're done talking. I just want to hold you. Nothing else matters right now."

Turning a bit more in his arms, Catalina looked up into those vibrant eyes that had haunted her dreams for years. "Make love to me, Will. I don't care about anything else. Not when I can be with you."

In one swift, powerful move, he had her straddling his lap. Catalina hissed a breath when her ankle bumped his thigh.

"Dammit. Sorry, Cat."

She offered him a smile, stroking the pad of her thumb along the worry lines between his brows. "I'm fine," she assured him as she slid the ties at the side of her dress free. "I don't want to think about my injury, why we're stuck here or what's waiting for us when we get back. All I want is to feel you against me."

Will took in the sight of her as she continued to work out of her clothing. When his hands spanned her waist, she arched against his touch.

He leaned forward, resting his forehead against her chest as he whispered, "You're more than I deserve and everything I've ever wanted."

Framing his face with her hands, Catalina lifted his head until she could look him in the eyes. "No more talking," she reminded him with a soft kiss to his lips. "No more talking tonight."

Tomorrow, or whenever they were able to get off this island, she'd tell him about his father. But for now, she'd take this gift she'd been given and worry about the ugly truth, and how they would handle it, later.

Fifteen

By the second day, Catalina still hadn't told Will the truth. How could she reveal such a harsh reality when they'd been living in passionate bliss on a beautiful island in some fantasy?

They'd both fiddled with the radio and tried their cell phones from various spots on the island, but nothing was going through. She wasn't going to panic quite yet. They had plenty of food and for a bit, she could pretend this was a dream vacation with the man she'd fallen in love with.

Will rolled over in bed, wrapping his arm around her and settling against her back. "I'd like to say I can't wait to get off this island, but waking up with you in my arms is something I could get used to."

His husky tone filled her ear. The coarse hair on his chest tickled her back, but she didn't mind. She loved the feel of Will next to her.

"I'm getting pretty spoiled, too." She snuggled deeper into his embrace. "I'm never going to want to leave."

"Maybe that's how I want you to be," he replied, nipping her shoulder.

"We can't stay here forever," she laughed.

"As long as you don't leave Alma, I'm okay with going back."

A sliver of reality crept back in. Catalina shifted so that she could roll over in his arms and face him.

"I don't plan on working as a maid forever," she informed him, staring into his eyes. "And after what you told me about your father, I think it's best if I don't work there anymore. I can't work for a man who completely altered my future. I stayed with James because I adore him and I moved on to Patrick because I needed the job, but now that I know the full truth, I can't stay there."

Will propped himself up on his elbow and peered down at her. "I understand, but stay in Alma. Stay with me."

"And do what?" she asked, already knowing this conversation was going to divide them. "I have goals, Will. Goals that I can't ignore simply because we're... I don't even know what this is between us right now."

"Do you need a label?" he asked.

Part of her wanted to call this something. Maybe then she could justify her feelings for a man who'd let her go so easily before.

She had no idea what she was going to do once she got back to Alma. Working for Patrick was not going to happen. She'd put up with his arrogance for too long. Thankfully she'd only worked for him a short time because up until recently, James had been the one occupying the Playa del Onda home. Catalina had had a hard enough time working for Patrick knowing what she did about her mother, but now knowing he'd manipulated his son and crushed their relationship, Catalina couldn't go back there. Never again.

So where did that leave her? She didn't think she was quite ready to head out with her designs and start pursuing her goal. She had a few more things she'd like to complete before she made that leap.

"What's going through your mind?" Will asked, studying her face.

"You know the sewing set you got me?"

Will nodded.

"You have no idea how much that touched me." Catalina raked her hand through his blond hair and trailed her fingertips down his jaw, his neck. "I've been sewing in my spare time. Making things for myself, for my mother. It's been such a great escape and when I saw what you'd gotten me, I…"

Catalina shook her head and fell back against the bed. She stared up at the ceiling and wished she could find the right words to tell him how much she appreciated the gift.

"So you're saying it was a step up from the flowers?" he joked.

Shifting her gaze to him, her heart tightened at his playful smile. "I may have cried," she confessed. "That was the sweetest gift ever."

Will settled over her, his hands resting on either side of her head. "It was meant more as a joke," he said with a teasing smile. "And maybe I wanted to remind you of what we did in the utility room."

Cat smacked his chest. "As if I could've forgotten. That's all I could think about and you know it."

He gave her a quick kiss before he eased back. "It's all I could think of, too, if that helps."

Catalina wrapped her arms around his neck, threading her fingers through his hair. "What are we going to do when we get back?"

"We're going to take this one day at a time because I'm not screwing this up again."

"We can't seem to function in normal life."

Will's forehead rested against hers as he let out a sigh. "Trust me, Cat. I've fought too hard to get you back. I'm going to fight just as hard to keep you."

Catalina prayed that was true, because all too soon she was going to have to reveal the final secret between them if she wanted a future with this man.

Cat lay on the deck sunbathing in that skimpy bikini, which was positively driving him out of his mind. Right now he didn't give a damn that the radio was beyond repair or that their phones weren't getting a signal. For two days they'd made love, stayed in bed and talked, spending nearly every single moment together.

Perhaps that's why he was in such agony. He knew exactly what that lush body felt like against his own. He knew how amazingly they fit together with no barriers between them.

Will couldn't recall the last time he'd taken this much time away from work. Surprisingly he wasn't getting twitchy. He'd set his plan into motion a couple months ago for Rowling Energy and it shouldn't be too much longer before everything he'd ever wanted clicked into place like a perfectly, methodically plotted puzzle.

Will folded his arms behind his head and relaxed on the seat opposite Cat. But just as he closed his eyes, the soft hum of an engine had him jumping to his feet.

"Do you hear that?" he asked, glancing toward the horizon.

Cat sat up, her hand shielding her eyes as she glanced in the same direction. "Oh, there's another boat."

Will knew that boat and he knew who would be on board. Good thing his brother hadn't left to go back to training for football yet because that meant he could come to their rescue. Which was what he was doing right now.

"Looks like our fairy tale is over," Catalina muttered.

He glanced her way. "It's not over," he corrected. "It's just beginning."

As James's yacht closed the distance between them, Will slid his shoes back on. "Stay here. I'll wave James to the other side of the dock where the damage isn't as bad. And I'll carry you on board once we're secure."

Cat rolled her eyes and reached for her wrap draped across the back of the white sofa. "I can walk, Will. My ankle is sore, but it's much better than it was."

Will wasn't going to argue. He'd win in the end regardless.

As soon as James was near enough, Will hopped up onto the dock and made his way toward the other end. By the time James came to a stop, Bella was at his side, a worried look etched across her face.

"Coast guard has arrived," James said, coming up behind his wife.

"I figured you'd come along sooner or later," Will replied.

James took in the damage to the dock and the yacht. "Damn, you've got a mess. That must've been one hell of a storm. It rained and there was some thunder and wind in Alma, but no damage."

"Let me go get our things," Will told his brother. "I need to carry Cat, too. She's hurt."

"Oh no," Bella cried. "What happened?"

"I fell."

Will turned to see Cat leaning over the side of the yacht. "You're supposed to be sitting down," he called back.

"I'm fine. I will need some help off this thing, but I can walk if I go slow."

Will shook his head. "I'll carry her," he told his brother. "Give me a few minutes to get our personal stuff gathered."

Once they transferred everything Will and Cat needed to his brother's yacht and Will carried a disgruntled Cat on board, they were ready to head out. The trip back to Alma was filled with questions from Bella and James. Their worry was touching and Will actually found himself loving this newfound bond he and his brother shared. This is what he'd been missing for years. This is what their grief had torn apart after their mother had died. But now they were slowly making their way back to each other.

"I wasn't quite sure which island you went to," James said as they drew nearer to Alma's coastline. "I went to two last night and had to start again today when I couldn't find you."

"Did you tell anyone what was going on?" Will asked.

"No." James maneuvered the boat and pulled back on the throttle. "Bella and I are the only ones who know where you were."

Will was relieved nobody else knew. He didn't want to share Cat or their relationship with anyone just yet. He wanted to bask in their privacy for a bit longer.

"Dammit," James muttered as they neared what was supposed to be a private dock where Alma's rich and famous kept their boats. "The damn press is here."

"What for?" Cat asked, her eyes widening.

"There were a few reporters here when I left earlier,"

James stated as he steered the yacht in. "They were speculating because Will's yacht had been missing for a few days and they knew a storm had come through. They asked me where you were and I ignored them."

Will groaned. So much for that privacy he'd been clinging to. "Don't they have anything better to cover? Like the fact Juan Carlos is going to be crowned king in a few weeks? Do they seriously have to focus on me?"

Cat's eyes remained fixed on the throng of reporters and cameras turning in their direction.

Will crouched down before her seat and smoothed her hair back from her face. "Ignore them. No matter what they say, do not make a comment. They'll forget about this by tomorrow and we can move on."

Her eyes sought his and she offered him a smile. "Ignore them. That I can do."

Will stood back up and offered her his hand. "I'm going to at least put my arm around you so you can put some of your weight on me. Anyone looking will just think I'm helping you."

"I'll carry her bag," Bella offered. "I'll go first. Maybe they'll focus on James and me. I can always just start discussing my upcoming fund-raiser for my foundation next weekend. I'm okay with yanking the reporters' chains, too."

Will couldn't help but laugh at Bella's spunk. She was the perfect match for his brother.

As they made their way down the dock, Will kept his arm secured around Cat's waist. James and Bella took the lead, holding hands as they wedged through the sea of nosy people.

The reporters seemed to all start shouting at once.

"Where have you been for three days?"

"Was your yacht damaged by the storm?"

"Were you stranded somewhere?"

"Who is with you, Will?"

The questions kept coming as Will tried to shield Cat from the press. The whispers and murmurs infuriated him. Seriously? Wasn't there other newsworthy stuff happening in Alma right now? Dammit, this was one major drawback to being a wealthy, well-known businessman. And if he thought for a second he could have any privacy with Cat now that they were back, he was living in a fantasy.

When he heard someone say the word "staff" he clenched his jaw. He wouldn't respond. That's what they wanted: some type of reaction. He heard his father's name and for reasons unbeknownst to Will, the gossipmongers were starting to piece things together rather quickly. Where the hell would they have seen Cat? On occasion his father would allow a few press members to attend certain parties thrown by the Rowlings if there was a charity involved. Cat had been James's maid, too, though.

Will groaned as he kept his sights on his brother's back as the foursome pushed through to the waiting car in the distance. They couldn't get there fast enough for Will.

"Is your mistress a member of your family's staff, Mr. Rowling?"

The rude question had Cat stiffening at his side. "Keep going," he murmured. "Almost there."

"Wasn't she working for your brother?"

"Is she on Patrick's staff?"

"How long have you been seeing your father's maid?"

"Weren't you just engaged to your brother's wife?"

"What does your father think about you and his maid?"

Will snapped. "This isn't like that. You're all making a mistake."

Catalina's gasp had him jerking his gaze toward her. "Dammit," he muttered beneath his breath. "You know that's not what I mean."

Those damn words echoed from the last time he'd said them to her. And this time they were just as damaging when taken out of context.

Easing back from his side, Cat kept her eyes on his. "I'm not sure, Will. Because only moments ago you said ignore them and you said we'd take this one day at a time. We've only been back in Alma five minutes and you're already referring to me as a mistake."

Will raked a hand through his hair. From the corner of his eye he spotted James and Bella standing close. For once the reporters weren't saying a word. They waited, no doubt hoping to really get something juicy for their headlines.

"Marry me."

Okay, he hadn't meant to blurt that out there, but now that the words hovered between them, he wasn't sorry. Maybe Cat would see just how serious he was about them.

"Marry you?" she asked, her brows drawn in. "You're not serious."

He stepped forward and took her hand. "We are not a mistake, Cat. You know we're perfect together. Why wouldn't you?"

Cat stared back at him, and then shook her head and let out a soft laugh. "This is ridiculous. You don't mean this proposal so why would you do this to me? Why would you ask that in front of all these people? To prove them wrong? Because you got caught with the maid and you're trying to glamorize it?"

"Dammit, Cat, this has nothing to do with anyone else. We can talk later, in private."

He didn't want to hash this out here in front of the press. And he sure as hell didn't want to sound as if he was backpedaling because he'd chosen the worst possible time to blurt out a proposal.

Crossing her arms over her chest, she tipped her chin up just a notch, but enough for him to know she was good and pissed. "Would you have proposed to me if all of these people hadn't been around? Later tonight when we were alone, would you have asked me to marry you?"

Will gritted his teeth, clenched his fists at his side and honestly had no reply. He had absolutely no idea what to say. He didn't want to have such an intimate talk in front of the whole country, because that's exactly what was happening. The press would no doubt splash this all over the headlines.

"That's what I thought." Cat's soft tone was full of hurt. "I'd say it's officially over between us."

When she turned, she winced, but just as Will reached to help her, Bella stepped forward and slowly ushered Cat to the car. James moved in next to Will and ordered the press away. Will didn't hear much, didn't comprehend what was going on because in the span of just a few minutes, he'd gone from deliriously happy and planning his future, to seeing that future walk away from him after he'd hurt her, called her a mistake, once again.

This time, he knew there would be no winning her back.

Sixteen

"What the hell is this?"

Will turned away from his office view to face his father, who stood on the other side of his desk with a folder in his hand. Will had been waiting for this moment. But he hadn't expected to feel this enormous pit of emptiness inside.

"I see you received the notice regarding your shares in Rowling Energy." Will folded his arms across his chest and leveled his father's gaze. "Your votes in the company are no longer valid. I held an emergency meeting with the other stockholders and we came to the decision."

Patrick's face reddened. "How dare you. What kind of son did I raise that he would turn around and treat his father like this?"

"You raised the son who fought for what he wanted." Will's blood pressure soared as he thought of all he'd lost and all he was still fighting for. "You raised a son who watched his father put business first, above family, and to hell with the rest of the world. I'm taking Rowling Energy into new territory and I need sole control. I'm done being jerked around by you."

Patrick rested his palms on the desk and leaned in. "No, you'd rather be jerked around by my maid. You two made quite a scene yesterday—it made headlines. You're becoming an embarrassment and tarnishing the Rowling name."

Will laughed. "What I do in my personal life is not your concern. You poked your nose in years ago when you threatened to dismiss Catalina if I didn't dump her. I won't be manipulated ever again and you will leave Cat alone. If I even think you've tried to—"

"Knock off the threats," his father shouted as he pushed off the desk. "Your little maid quit on me and has really left me in a bind. If you were smart, you'd stay away from her. You two get cozy and she quits. I don't believe in coincidences. Those Iberra women are nothing but gold diggers."

Will stood up straighter, dropped his arms to his sides. "What did you say?"

Patrick waved a hand in the air, shaking his head. "Forget it."

"No. You said 'those Iberra women.' What did you mean?"

Will knew Cat's mother had worked for Patrick years ago. Maria had been around when James and Will had been young, when their mother was still alive.

"What did Maria do that you would call her a gold digger?" Will asked when his father remained silent.

Still, Patrick said nothing.

Realization dawned on Will. "No. Tell me you didn't have an affair with Maria."

"Every man has a moment of weakness," Patrick stated simply. "I expect this past weekend was yours."

Rage boiled to the surface. Will clenched his fists. "You slept with Cat's mother while my mother was still alive? Did Mum know about the affair?"

The thought of his sweet, caring mother being betrayed tore through Will's heart. Part of him prayed she never knew the ugly acts his father had committed.

"She found out the day she died." Patrick let out a sigh, his eyes darting to the ground. "We were arguing about it when she left that night."

For once the great Patrick Rowling looked defeated. Which was nothing less than he deserved. Will's heart was absolutely crushed. He reached out, gripped the back of his desk chair and tried to think rationally here. Finding out your father had an affair with the mother of a woman you had fallen for was shocking enough. But to add to the intensity, his mother had died as a result of the affair.

Dread settled deep in Will's his gut. Did Cat know of this affair? Surely not. Surely she would have told him or at least hinted at the knowledge. Would this crush her, too?

"Get out," Will said in a low, powerful tone as he kept his eyes on the blotter on his desk. "Get the hell out of my office and be glad my freezing your voting rights in this company is all I'm doing to you."

Patrick didn't move. Will brought his gaze up and glared at the man he'd once trusted.

"You have one minute to be out of this building or I'll call security."

"I never thought you'd turn on me," his father replied.

"I turned on you four years ago when you threatened the woman I love."

Will hadn't meant to declare his love for Cat, but it felt good to finally let the words out. And now more than ever he wasn't giving up. He was going to move heaven and earth to win her back because he did love her. He'd always loved her if he was honest with himself. And he wanted a life with her now more than ever.

Bella was having a fund-raiser this coming weekend and Will knew he was going to need reinforcements. He wasn't letting Cat go. Not this time. Never again.

"I figured you'd be at work today." James sank down onto the chaise longue on his patio as Maisey played in her sandbox. "You look like hell, man."

Will shoved his hands in his pockets and glanced toward the ocean. "I feel like hell. Thanks for pointing it out."

"You still haven't talked to Catalina?"

Maisey squealed, threw her toy shovel and started burying her legs beneath the sand. Will watched his niece and wondered if there could ever be a family for Cat and him. She wanted a family and the more he thought of a life with her, the more he wanted the same thing.

"No, I haven't seen her." Will shifted his focus to his brother and took a seat on the edge of a chair opposite him. "Bella's fund-raiser is going to be at the Playa del Onda house this weekend, right?"

"Yes. Dad will be out of town and that house is perfect for entertaining. Why?"

"I want you to ask Cat to help with the staff there." Will held up a hand before his brother could cut him off. "I have my reasons, but I need your help in order to make this work."

James shook his head and stared down at his daughter for a minute before he looked back at Will. "This could blow up in your face."

Will nodded. "It's a risk I'm willing to take."

"What's in it for me?" James asked with a smirk.

Will laughed. Without even thinking twice, he unfastened the watch on his wrist and held it up. "This."

James's eyes widened. "I was joking."

"I'm not." Will reached out and placed the watch on the arm of his brother's chair. "You deserve it back. This has nothing to do with you helping me with Cat. The watch is rightfully yours."

James picked it up and gripped it in his hand. "We've really come a long way," he muttered.

Will had one more piece of business to take care of and he was not looking forward to this discussion at all. There was no way James knew of the affair or he definitely would've said something. Will really hated to crush his brother with the news, but James deserved to know.

"I need to tell you something." Will glanced at Maisey. "Is your nanny here or is Bella busy?"

James sat up in his seat, slid his watch on and swung his legs around to the deck. "Bella was answering emails, but she can watch Maisey. Is everything okay?"

Will shook his head. "Not really."

Worry and concern crossed James's face as he nodded. After taking Maisey inside, he returned moments later, closing the patio doors behind him.

"This must really be something if it has you this upset." James sat back down on the edge of his chair. "What's going on?"

Will took in a deep breath, blew it out and raked a hand through his hair. "This is harder than I thought," he said on a sigh. "Do you remember the night Mum died? Dad woke us and said she'd been in an accident?"

James nodded. "I heard them arguing earlier that evening. I was heading downstairs to get some water and heard them fighting so I went back upstairs."

Will straightened. "You heard them arguing?"

James nodded. "Dad raised his voice, and then Mum was crying and Dad was saying something else but in a lower tone. I didn't hear what all he said."

Will closed his eyes and wished like hell he could go back and...what? What could he have done differently? He'd been a kid. Even if James had gone downstairs and interrupted the fight, most likely their mother still would've walked out to get away from their father.

"What is it?" James prodded. "What aren't you telling me?"

Will opened his eyes and focused on his brother. "Dad had an affair. They were arguing about that."

"What?" James muttered a curse. "Has that man ever valued his family at all?"

"There's more." Will hesitated a moment, swallowed and pushed forward. "The affair was with Maria. Cat's mum."

Will started to wonder if James had heard him, but suddenly his brother jumped to his feet and let out a chain of curses that even had Will wincing. James kicked the leg of the chair, propped his hands on his hips and dropped his head between his shoulders.

"If I'd have gone downstairs that night..." he muttered.

"Mum still would've left," Will said softly. "We can't go back in time and you're not to blame. Our dad is the one whose selfish needs stole our mother. He crushed her. She would've done anything for him and he threw it all away."

James turned. "Does Cat know this?"

Shaking his head, Will came to his feet. "I doubt it. She's never said a word to me."

"Do you think once she knows the truth she'll take you back?"

Yeah, the odds were more than stacked against him, but he refused to back down. Nobody would steal his life again. And Cat was his entire life.

"I don't even know what to say about this," James said, staring out to the ocean. "I never had much respect for Dad, but right now I hate that man."

"I've made his life hell." Will was actually pleased with the timing. "As CEO of Rowling Energy, I've frozen his shares. He can no longer vote on any company matters that come before the board."

James smiled. "If this action were directed to an enemy, dear old Dad would be proud of your business tactics."

"Yeah," Will agreed, returning the grin. "He's not too proud right now, though. But I have more pressing matters to tend to."

James reached out, patted Will on the back. "I'll do what I can where Cat is concerned. I know what this is like to be so torn over a woman."

Torn wasn't even the word.

"I never thought either of us would fall this hard." Will pulled in a deep breath. "Now we need Bella to convince Cat to work the party. I can take it from there. I just need you guys to get her there."

Seventeen

If Catalina didn't adore Bella and her valiant efforts to raise money for the Alma Wildlife Conservation Society which she'd recently founded, Catalina wouldn't have stepped foot back into this house.

But Patrick was out of town and Bella and James had caught Catalina at a weak moment, offering her an insane amount of money to help set up for the event.

In the past week since she'd last seen Will, she'd not heard one word from him. Apparently she wasn't worth fighting for after all. Not that she would have forgiven him, but a girl likes to at least know she's worth something other than a few amazing sexual encounters.

Catalina hurried through the house, hoping to get everything set up perfectly before the first guests arrived.

Okay, fine. There was only one person on the guest list she was trying like hell to avoid.

She'd spent this past week furiously working on her

final designs. She didn't have the amount of money saved up that she wanted before she left Alma, but it would just have to be enough. Alma had nothing left to offer her. Not anymore.

Catalina took a final walkthrough, adjusting one more floral arrangement on the foyer table before she was satisfied with everything. She'd already double-checked with the kitchen to make sure the food was ready and would be served according to the set schedule. She'd also told Bella she would be back around midnight to clean up. There was just no way she could stay during the party. That had been her only condition for working tonight, and thankfully Bella had agreed.

Catalina checked her watch. Only thirty minutes until guests were due to arrive. Time to head out. She'd opted to park near the side entrance off the utility room. Just as she turned into the room to grab her purse and keys, she ran straight into a very hard, very familiar chest.

Closing her eyes, she tried like hell not to breathe in, but Will's masculine aroma enveloped her just as his strong arms came around to steady her.

"Running away?" he whispered in her ear.

Knowing she'd never get out without talking, Catalina shored up all of her courage and lifted her gaze to his. "I'm not the one who usually runs."

Keeping his aqua eyes on her, Will reached around, slammed the door and flicked the lock. "Neither of us is getting out of here until we talk."

"I don't need you to hold onto me," she told him, refusing to glance away. No way was he keeping the upper hand here just because her heart was in her throat.

"I want to make sure you'll stay put."

He dropped his hands but didn't step back. The

warmth from his body had hers responding. She wished she didn't fall so easily into the memories of their love-making, wished she didn't get swept away by such intriguing eyes. Even through their rocky moments, Catalina couldn't deny that all the good trumped the bad…at least in her heart.

"I'll stay." She stepped back until she was flat against the door. "If I don't listen now, I know you'll show up at my apartment. Might as well get this over with."

Why couldn't he be haggard or have dark circles beneath his eyes? Had he not been losing sleep over the fact he'd been a jerk? Why did he have to be so damn sexy all the time and why couldn't she turn off her hormones around this man who constantly hurt her?

"There's so much I want to say," he muttered as he ran a hand over his freshly shaven jaw. "I don't know where to start."

Catalina tapped her watch. "Better hurry. The party starts soon."

"I don't give a damn about that party. I already gave Bella a check for the foundation."

"Of course you did," she muttered. "What do you want from me, Will?"

He stepped forward until her body was firmly trapped between his and the door. Placing a hand on either side of her head, he replied, "Everything."

Oh, mercy. She wasn't going to be able to keep up this courage much longer if he kept looking at her like that, if he touched her or used those charming words.

"You can't have everything." She licked her lips and stared up at him. "You can't treat everything like a business deal, only giving of yourself when it's convenient for you or makes you look good in the public eye."

Will smoothed her hair away from her face and she

simply couldn't take it anymore. She placed her hands on his chest and shoved him back, slipping past him to get some breathing room before she lost her mind and clung to him.

"I'm actually glad you cornered me," she went on, whirling around to face him. "I didn't want to run into you tonight, but we both need closure. I don't want to leave Alma with such awkwardness between us."

"Leave Alma," he repeated. "You're not leaving Alma."

Catalina laughed. "You know you can't control everyone, right? I am leaving. In two weeks, actually. My mother and I have tickets and we're heading to Milan."

"What's in Milan?"

Catalina tucked her hair behind her ears and crossed her arms. "My new life. I've been working for nearly four years and I'm finally ready to take my clothing designs and see what I can do in the world. I may not get far, but I'm going to try."

Will's brows drew in as he listened. Catalina actually liked the fact that she'd caught him off guard. He'd been knocking the air out of her lungs for a good while now and it was only appropriate she return the favor.

"I know you're angry with me for blurting out the proposal in front of such an audience, but you have to listen to me now."

"I'll listen, but you're wasting your time if you're trying to convince me of anything. We're not meant to be, Will. We've tried, and we weren't successful either time. I don't want to keep fighting a losing battle."

"I've never lost a battle in my life," he informed her as he took a step closer. "I don't intend to lose this one."

"You already lost," she whispered. "On the island we were so happy and for that time I really thought we could come back here and build on that. But once again, I was naïve where you were concerned. As soon as we stepped foot back in Alma, you turned into that take-charge man who didn't want to look like a fool in front of the cameras. You were embarrassed to be seen with the maid, and then when you realized just how much of a jerk you were being, you opted to propose? Did you honestly think I'd accept that?"

Will was close enough to touch, but he kept his hands propped on his hips. "I reacted without thinking. Dammit, Cat we'd just had the best few days together and I was scared, all right? Everything about us terrifies me to the point I can't think straight. I've never wanted anything or anyone the way I want you and I've never been this afraid of losing what I love forever."

Catalina gasped. He didn't just say... No, he didn't love her. He was using those pretty words to control her, to trick her into...

What? What was his end game here?

"You don't love me, Will." Oh, how she wished he did, but that was still the naïve side of her dreaming. "You love power."

"I won't deny power is important to me. But that also means I can use that power to channel some pretty damn intense emotions." He leaned in, close enough for her to feel his breath on her face, yet he still didn't touch her. "And I love you more than any business deal, more than any merger or sale. I love you, Catalina."

She didn't want to hear this. He'd used her full name so she knew he was serious, or as serious as he could be.

"I don't want this," she murmured, trying to look away, but trapped by the piercing gaze. "I have plans, Will, and I can't hinge my entire life around a man who may or may not put me above his career."

And even if she could give in and let him have her heart, she carried this secret inside of her that would surely drive another sizeable wedge between them.

"Listen to me." He eased back, but reached out and placed his hands on either side of her face. "Hear every single word I'm about to tell you. For the past four years I've fought to get you back. At first I'll admit it was because my father wanted something else for my life and I was being spiteful, but the longer you and I were apart, the more I realized there was an empty ache inside of me that couldn't be filled. I poured myself into work, knowing the day would come when I'd take over Rowling Energy. Even through all of that, I was plotting to get you back."

He stared at her, his thumb stroking back and forth along the length of her jawline as if he was putting her into some type of trance.

"Just the thought of you with another man was crushing, but I knew if I didn't fight for you, for us, then you'd settle down and I'd lose you forever. I've always put you first, Cat. Always. Even when we weren't together, I was working my way back to you."

When she started to glance away, he tipped her head up, forcing her to keep her eyes on his. "You think I was working this long to win you back just to have sex with you? I want the intimacy, I want the verbal sparring matches we get into, I want to help you pick up those little seashells along the beach and I want to wake up with you beside me every day for the rest of my life. Rowling Energy and all I have there mean nothing in the grand scheme of things. I want the money and the power, but I want you more than any of that."

Catalina chewed on her bottom lip, trying to force her chin to stop quivering. She was on the verge of losing it and once the dam burst on her tears, she might never regain control.

"Before you decide, I don't want anything coming between us again," he went on. "I need to tell you something that is quite shocking and I just discovered myself."

Catalina reached up, gripped his wrists and eased his hands away from her face. She kept hold of him, but remained still. "What is it?"

"There's no easy way to tell you this without just saying it."

Fear pumped through her as her heart kicked up the pace. What on earth was he going to reveal? Whatever it was, it was a big deal. And once he told her his shocking news, she had a bombshell of her own to drop because she also couldn't move forward, with or without him, and still keep this secret.

"I found out that my father and your mother had an affair."

When Catalina stared at him for a moment, his eyes widened and he stepped back. She said nothing, but the look on his face told her all she needed to know.

"You already knew?" he asked in a whisper. "Didn't you?"

Cat nodded. Will's heart tightened. How had she known? How could she keep something so important from him?

"You've known awhile," he said, keeping his eyes on her unsurprised face. "How long?"

Cat blinked back the moisture that had gathered in her dark eyes. "Four years."

Rubbing the back of his neck, Will glanced down at

the floor. He couldn't look at her. Couldn't believe she'd keep such a monumental secret from him.

"I didn't know when we were together," she told him. "My mom told me after we broke up. I was so upset and she kept telling me how the Rowling men... Never mind. It's not important."

Everything about this was important, yet the affair really had nothing to do with how he felt for Cat. The sins of their parents didn't have to trickle down to them and ruin their happiness.

"I still can't believe you didn't say anything."

Cat turned, walked to the door and stared out into the backyard. Will took in her narrow shoulders, the exposed nape of her neck. She wasn't wearing her typical black shirt and pants. Right now she had on a pair of flat sandals, a floral skirt and some type of fitted shirt that sat right at the edge of her shoulders. She looked amazing and she was just out of his reach, physically and emotionally.

"I wanted to tell you on the island," she said, keeping her back to him. "I tried once, but we got sidetracked. That's an excuse. I should've made you listen, but we were so happy and there was no such thing as reality during those few days. I just wanted to stay in that euphoric moment."

He couldn't fault her for that because he'd felt the exact same way.

"There's just so much against us, Will." She turned back around and the lone tear on her cheek gutted him. "Sometimes people can love each other and still not be together. Sometimes love isn't enough and people just need to go their own way."

Will heard what she was saying, but how could he not hone in on the one main point to her farewell speech?

"You love me?" He couldn't help but smile as he crossed to her. "Say it, Cat. I want to hear the words."

She shook her head. "It doesn't mean anything."

"Say it." His hands settled around her waist as he pulled her flush against him. "Now."

"I love you, Will, but—"

He crushed his lips to hers. Nothing else mattered after those life-altering words. Nothing she could say would erase the fact that she loved him and he loved her, and he'd be damn it if he would ever let her walk away.

Her body melted against his as her fingers curled around his biceps. Will lifted his mouth from hers, barely.

"Don't leave, Cat," he murmured against her lips. "Don't leave Alma. Don't leave me."

"I can't give up who I am, Will." She closed her eyes and sighed. "No matter how much I love you, I can't give up everything I've worked for and I wouldn't expect you to give up your work for me. We have different goals in different directions."

The fear of losing her, the reality that if he didn't lay it all on the line, then she would be out of his life for good hit him hard.

"I'm coming with you."

Cat's eyes flew open as Will tipped his head back to see her face better. "What?"

"I meant what I said. I won't give you up and you're more to me than any business. But I can work from anywhere and I can fly to Alma when I need to."

"You can't be serious." Panic flooded her face. "This is rushed. You can't expect me to just say okay and we'll be on our way to happily-ever-after. It's too fast."

Will laughed. "I've known you since you were a little girl. I dated you four years ago and last weekend you spent nearly three days in my bed. You said you love me and I love the hell out of you and you think this is too fast? If we move any slower we'll be in a nursing home by the time you wear my ring on your finger."

"I can't think." Once again she pushed him aside and moved past him. "I can't take all this in. I mean, your dad and my mom…all of the things that have kept us apart. And then you corner me in a laundry room of all places to tell me you want me forever."

"So we don't do things the traditional way." He came up behind her, gripped her shoulders and kissed the top of her head. "I'm done with being by the book and boring. I want adventure, I want to be on a deserted island with the only woman in the world who can make me angry, laugh and love the way you do. I want to take care of you, I want to wear out the words *I love you* and I want to have no regrets from here on out where we are concerned."

Cat eased back against him, her head on his shoulder. "I want to believe all of that is possible. I want to hold on to the hope that I can still fulfill my dreams and I can have you. But I won't give up myself, no matter how much I love you, Will."

Wrapping his arms around her waist, he leaned his cheek on her head. "I wouldn't ask you to give up anything. I just didn't want you leaving Alma without me. We can live wherever you want. I have a jet, I have a yacht…well, I'll have a new one soon. I can travel where I need to be for work and I can take you where you need to go in order to fulfill this goal of yours. I want to be with you every step of your journey."

"I want to do it on my own," she stated, sliding her hands over his.

"I wouldn't dream of interfering," he replied. "I'll

support you in any way you need. I'll be the silent financial backer or I'll be the man keeping your bed warm at night and staying out of the business entirely. The choice is yours."

Cat turned in his arms, laced her hands behind his neck and stared up at him. "Tell me this is real. Tell me you don't hate me for keeping the secret and that you will always make me first in your life."

"It's real." He kissed her forehead. "I could never hate you." He kissed her nose. "And you'll never question again whether you're first in my life."

He slid his mouth across hers, gliding his hands down her body to the hem of her shirt. Easing the hem up, he smoothed his palms up over her bare skin, pleased when she shivered beneath his touch.

"Are you seriously trying to seduce me in a laundry room all while your sister-in-law is throwing a party to raise money for her foundation a few feet away?"

Will laughed as his lips traveled down the column of her throat. "I'm not trying. I'm about to succeed."

Cat's body arched back as her fingers threaded through his hair. "I hope no partygoers take a stroll through the backyard and glance in the window of the door," she panted when his hands brushed the underside of her breasts.

"We already made headlines." He jerked the shirt up and over her head, flinging it to the side without a care. "Another one won't matter at this point."

"What will your brother think if you don't show at the party?"

Will shrugged. "James is pretty smart. I'd say he'll know exactly where I am."

Cat started working on the buttons of his shirt and

soon sent the shirt and his jacket to the floor. "We still don't have a solid plan for our future."

Hoisting her up, Will sat her on the counter and settled between her legs. "I know how the next several minutes are going to play out. Beyond that I don't care so long as you're with me."

Will kissed her once more and eased back. "But I already have the perfect wedding present for you."

Cat laughed as her arms draped over his shoulders. "And what's that?"

"A maid. You'll not lift a finger for me ever. I want you to concentrate on your design career and the babies we're going to have in the future."

When Cat's smile widened and she tightened her hold on him, Will knew the four years he'd worked on getting back to her were worth it. Everything he'd sacrificed with his father and personal life was worth this moment, knowing he was building a future with the only woman he'd ever loved.

* * * * *

If you're on Twitter, tell us what you think of
Harlequin Desire! #harlequindesire

COMING NEXT MONTH FROM

HARLEQUIN *Desire*

Available October 6, 2015

#2401 A CONTRACT ENGAGEMENT • by Maya Banks

In this reader-favorite story, billionaire businessman Evan Ross has special terms for Celia Taylor, the sexy ad executive desperate to seal a career-making deal. But she's turning the tables with demands of her own...

#2402 STRANDED WITH THE BOSS

Billionaires and Babies • by Elizabeth Lane

Early tragedy led billionaire Dragan to steer clear of children. But could a spunky redhead—who's suing his company!—and her twin toddlers melt his frozen heart when they're stranded together in a winter cabin?

#2403 PURSUED

The Diamond Tycoons • by Tracy Wolff

Nic Durand had a one-night stand with the reporter exposing corruption in his company. Now she's having his child. She may be set on bringing him down, but he'll pursue her until he has her right where he wants her!

#2404 A ROYAL TEMPTATION

Dynasties: The Montoros • by Charlene Sands

When Princess Portia Lindstrom shows up at his coronation, it's love at first sight for King Juan Carlos. But soon her family's explosive secret could force the unwavering royal to choose between his country's future and his own.

#2405 FALLING FOR HER FAKE FIANCÉ

The Beaumont Heirs • by Sarah M. Anderson

Frances Beaumont needs a fortune. CEO Ethan Logan needs a Beaumont to give him credibility when he takes over the family brewery. Can this engagement of convenience lead to the real deal?

#2406 HIS 24-HOUR WIFE

The Hawke Brothers • by Rachel Bailey

Their spontaneous Vegas marriage should have ended the day after it began! But when they partner on a project, Adam and Callie must pretend they're still together to avoid a high-profile scandal. Will they soon want more than a short-term solution?

He was the most beautiful man she'd ever seen.

Desi Maddox knew that sounded excessive, melodramatic even, but the longer she stood there staring at him, the more convinced she became.

His emerald gaze met hers over the sea of people stretching between them and her knees trembled. Her heart raced and her palms grew damp with the force of her reaction to a man she'd never seen before and more than likely would never see again.

It was a deflating thought, and exactly what she needed to remind herself of what she was doing here among the best and brightest of San Diego's high society. Scoping out hot men was definitely not what her boss was paying her for. Unfortunately.

Wanting to free up her hands, she turned to place her glass on the empty tray of yet another passing waiter. As she turned back, though, her eyes once again met dark green ones. And, this time, the man they belonged to was only a couple of feet away.

She didn't know whether to run or rejoice.

In the end, she just stared—stupefied—up into his too-gorgeous face and tried to think of something to say that wouldn't make her sound like a total moron. Her usually quick mind was a blank, filled with nothing but images of high cheekbones. Shaggy black hair that fell over his forehead. Wickedly gleaming eyes. The sensuous mouth turned up in a wide, charming smile. Broad shoulders. And height. He was so tall she was forced to look up, despite the fact that she stood close to six feet in her four-inch heels.

"You look thirsty," he said, and—of course—his voice matched the rest of him. All deep and dark and husky and wickedly amused. "I'm Nic, by the way."

"I'm Desi." She held out her hand. He took it, but instead of shaking it as she'd expected, he held it as he gently stroked his thumb across the back.

It was so soft, so intimate, so not what she'd been expecting, that for long seconds she didn't know what to do. A tiny voice inside her was whispering for her to escape from the attraction holding them in thrall. But it was drowned out by the heat, the *sizzle*, that arced between them like lightning.

"Would you like to dance, Desi?" he asked.

She should say no. But even as the thought occurred to her, even knowing that she might very well get burned before the night was over, she nodded.

Don't miss PURSUED
by New York Times *bestselling author Tracy Wolff,*
available October 2015 wherever
Harlequin® Desire books and ebooks are sold.

www.Harlequin.com

HDEXP0915

THE WORLD IS BETTER WITH

Romance

Harlequin has everything from contemporary, passionate and heartwarming to suspenseful and inspirational stories.

Whatever your mood, we have a romance just for you!